PAST BETRAYALS

As soon as Jon Farrell realized Julia had fallen in love with him, he broke off their relationship and returned to his work in the Middle East. When Jon's best friend, Danny, proposed a marriage of friendship, Julia accepted and pushed Jon to the back of her mind, only to find herself widowed a few months later. Then Jon returned and Julia discovered her love for him remained unchanged, despite his past betrayal. She was to learn that Jon had a secret — but was it his, or Danny's?

GIULIA GRAY

PAST BETRAYALS

Complete and Unabridged

LINFORD
Leicester

First published in Great Britain in 1991

First Linford Edition
published 1997

British Library CIP Data

Gray, Giulia
    Past betrayals.—Large print ed.—
    Linford romance library
    1. English fiction—20th century
    2. Large type books
    I. Title
    823.9'14 [F]

    ISBN 0–7089–5014–0

Published by
F. A. Thorpe (Publishing) Ltd.
Anstey, Leicestershire

Set by Words & Graphics Ltd.
Anstey, Leicestershire
Printed and bound in Great Britain by
T. J. Press (Padstow) Ltd., Padstow, Cornwall

This book is printed on acid-free paper

1

SO difficult to sleep without you beside me darling. . . . Funny how I got used to it in that short time — and you said it would never work! I've got your photo beside the bed but it's no substitute for the real thing. Must finish now — I'm going up country to the site at the crack of dawn tomorrow. Love and kisses, Danny.

The flimsy airmail paper caught quickly, the small bright flame burning fiercely then dying in a curl of smoke. For a moment Danny's words remained, a ghostly negative on the charred paper then the draught from the chimney scattered them to nothingness.

Julia Leyton leaned back on her heels and pushed the heavy wings of dark

1

chestnut hair behind her ears. Her throat felt dry and constricted but she wasn't going to cry, not now. For six months of widowhood she'd conformed to other peoples' ideas of how she should be acting, living, even feeling and it had left her feeling a hypocrite, unable to mourn Danny in her own way.

She had Danny's ring, his photo and their marriage certificate. Those were all she needed to carry on, to start living her own life again. However it had seemed to other people theirs had been no conventional love match.

It had been a 'marriage of convenience.' Julia smiled as she remembered Danny using the expression, "After all," he'd said persuasively, "my Italian Grandmama would have expected nothing else."

Danny had left a great gulf in her life. He'd been a close and loving friend, someone who'd cared for her, who was fun to be with and she missed him. The sadness was that she had loved her husband, but had never been in love with him, not like . . . but she wouldn't allow herself to think of that. Danny had convinced her what they'd had was enough.

Spending the last two weeks with Danny's family had made it worse. The only son in a close-knit Anglo-Italian family he'd been adored by his parents and his five elder sisters. They mourned him uninhibitedly and treated Julia's reserve with respectful incomprehension.

Julia had enjoyed the first noisy, child-filled week, but by the middle of the second week she was desperate to get home. The visit had confirmed her growing feeling that it was time to get back to work, pick up the pieces of her old life.

"But *cara mia*," Pia Leyton had protested, "you don't need to work: Danny left you well provided for. Sell your house, move closer to the family, we'll look after you. And who knows," her comfortable shoulders had lifted in

3

a disbelieving shrug, "there may be another man good enough for you one day."

Julia couldn't tell her mother-in-law there would never be another man, that she'd married Danny because the only man she'd ever loved had rejected her. And Danny, for good reasons of his own had proposed to her, married her, knowing that.

It was still difficult to take in that he was never coming back. He'd never hidden from her how dangerous his job was as a civil engineer in some of the toughest areas of the world, but even so, for him to be killed in a road accident thousands of miles away in the Middle East had come as a terrible shock.

Julia got to her feet with the innate grace which came with her height, wandering bare-foot to the french windows opening out on to the overgrown garden. She should have taken up her next-door neighbour's offer to mow the lawn while she

4

was away, especially as the man who normally did the garden for her was on holiday. The June roses had come and gone, the sight of the brown drooping dead heads made her fingers itch to tidy up. She turned the key, pushing open the double doors in her eagerness, then stopped with a chuckle as she glanced down at the clingy low-cut silk nightdress. No doubt George, her neighbour would appreciate it, but it was hardly the thing to go gardening in!

She'd felt so decisive, so certain that it was time to stop being Danny's widow and become Julia Leyton again when she'd arrived home last night but she hadn't been able to sleep. For hours she'd tossed and turned until finally, before dawn she'd come downstairs to burn the letters as a gesture of independence.

It had proved more difficult than she'd thought and Julia had tried to stiffen her resolve with a small glass of whisky from the bottle she kept for her father's visits. The unfamiliar spirit, after the long drive, had knocked her out and she'd woken at nine, cramped and stiff on the sofa.

The thin chime of the carriage clock on the mantelpiece startled her. Suddenly she was famished, the thought of sizzling bacon making her mouth water. First of all she'd make a list, get herself organised — then tomorrow she'd ring Sir Max, ask if there was still a place for her at Faulkner Engineering.

After Danny's death she'd resigned her job as personnel officer. His insurance had left her with no need to work, and she'd let herself be convinced that she should give up, despite her boss's protests. Her old job would be filled but perhaps she could go back on a consultancy basis.

The envelope from the letter she'd burned lay on the rug. Julia bent to pick it up and a colour snapshot dropped at her feet. Two men dressed in identical creased khaki posed against

6

a massive earth-moving machine, their eyes screwed up against the harsh desert light. Danny's tan emphasised his dark Latin good looks, crisp curly black hair, the flash of white teeth.

Julia winced: she'd forgotten this photograph, pushed the image of the other man to the back of her mind along with the feelings it evoked in her.

Jon Farrell was as fair as Danny was dark, a good six inches taller, altogether broader, loose-limbed against Danny's tautness. He was laughing, blue eyes alive with amusement, one arm thrown casually across the shorter man's shoulders. He and Danny had been Faulkner's two best engineers, and Sir Max tended to send them out as a team on the more difficult foreign assignments.

Who said the camera couldn't lie, Julia wondered bitterly, looking at Jon's laughing face. He had the reputation of being uncompromisingly honest — but that hadn't stopped him making love to her, then dropping her as soon as he'd realised the inconvenient intensity of her feelings for him. Danny, his best friend, had picked up the pieces.

Julia straightened, the hurt anger threatening to engulf her all over again. She'd loved him, slept with him because of that love, then he'd dumped her like a one-night stand . . .

She ripped the photo carefully down the centre. It was a lovely, characteristic photo of Danny. Julia tucked it into the corner of the mirror, then threw the other half into the grate and set a match to it.

One day she'd have to face Jon. After all, if she went back to Faulkner's it was inevitable they'd meet. But she'd never let him touch her again, physically or mentally.

The doorbell rang as she was half-way up the stairs. Puzzled Julia paused, stuffed the letters into a drawer in the hall, and forgetting how she was dressed, opened the door.

Jon Farrell stood on her doorstep,

hands jammed into the pockets of his old jeans, big shoulders hunched under the thin cotton of his white shirt. His denim blue gaze looked down into her shocked hazel eyes.

Julia stepped back sharply. For one mad moment she believed she'd conjured him up by burning his picture.

"Jon!" she croaked, every instinct screaming at her to slam the door in his face. But her body refused to respond.

The sort of life he lived, the stresses and climate had early on etched deep lines of experience under the arrogant cheekbones and down the sides of his nose, but even through the blur of shock Julia saw the marks of more recent strain. He looked older than his thirty-five years, light years away from the relaxed, smiling Jon of the photo.

The silence between them stretched on, heavy with the resonance of bitter memories. Julia saw his face change, the sun-bleached brows draw together over suddenly shuttered eyes. All at once she was aware of how she must look, tousled hair unbrushed, the thin silk nightdress moulding her body. For the first time in months she was acutely conscious of herself as a woman.

"You're rather late for the funeral." She threw the words at him like a weapon and had the fleeting satisfaction of seeing him flinch. "But then, you never turned up for the wedding either, did you?"

"If it will make you feel any better we can have a slanging match, but let's do it indoors." Jon glanced over his shoulder at her neighbour who was leaning on his lawnmower staring.

"Everything OK Julia?" George Whitcombe came across to ask. Before Julia could react Jon brushed past her into the hall.

She pulled herself together rapidly. "Thanks George . . . it's just a colleague of Danny's . . . Jon Farrell, you remember him. I wasn't expecting him," she gestured at the clinging

10

green silk, "as you can see!" George grinned in amiable appreciation as she shut the door.

Jon was in the living-room, one elbow on the mantelpiece as she'd so often seen him before. He looked totally at home in the house he and Danny had shared as bachelors. When Danny and Julia had married Jon had moved out to a houseboat he now used as a base on his rare visits to the UK.

"*Please* make yourself at home," Julia invited sarcastically. "Perhaps you'd like some coffee?"

"That might not be a bad idea — for both of us." Jon's eyes travelled meaningfully to the half-empty bottle of Scotch. She'd fallen asleep without putting the top back on and the smell of alcohol hung faintly in the air. "That's no answer Julia," he stated flatly, hard eyes raking her white face. His meaning was unmistakable.

"*I* don't have to justify myself to you." She snatched up the bottle, "But

11

if you must know, it's my father's Scotch. I merely had a nightcap, not most of the bottle!"

The anger helped her to cope with the shock of seeing him, helped drown the impact of his physical presence.

"I'm sorry, but you've got to admit . . . " Jon didn't sound either apologetic, or convinced. His eyes ranged round the room, and Julia saw it as he must: forgotten flowers dead in a vase, dust everywhere. Her daily had gone on holiday while Julia was away and the place looked neglected, unloved.

He shrugged, the slight movement drawing Julia's eyes to the play of muscle under the thin fabric of his shirt, the bleached blond hairs glistening on his forearm. His face may have changed but his long, work-honed body was still as lithe as a big cat's.

Despite her anger, aching yearning hit her, the simple desire to be held in the shelter of Jon's body, despite everything, to be back in his arms.

Nothing — the words he'd used like weapons to drive her away, her marriage to Danny — had stopped her loving him. She mustn't let him see it.

"I'm going to get dressed," Julia squared her shoulders, brought up her chin and met the full force of his critical stare. The moment of weakness had passed: he'd proved before that all he'd ever felt for her was physical desire.

"If you want coffee you know where the kitchen is — but drink it quickly." She added with as much indifference as she could muster, "I don't know why you came Jon, we've nothing to say to each other."

She walked out of the room, feeling his eyes burning down the length of her bare back to the curve of the green silk flaring over her hips. At the top of the stairs she paused, one hand on the door-jamb of the spare room, the room that had once been Jon's.

She had been going out with Jon for

two months. By the night he'd led her to this room she was head over heels in love with him, certain that the first man she'd slept with was the only man for her — and that he felt the same.

As she stood there it all came sweeping back. She'd woken to the memory of tenderness and incredible passion, reaching out to find the bed empty beside her.

"Jon?" she'd called, and he'd wandered in from the bathroom, pulling on a sweater, his face shuttered and cold.

"I've got to go out."

"But . . . where? It's Saturday — aren't you going to stay with me?"

"Don't get the wrong idea. Last night was good . . . "

"But? There has to be a 'but'."

"But let's not take this too seriously. We're both adults Julia. Making love to you was pleasurable, but that's all there was to it. I never made you any promises, don't go turning this into a big romance. Marriage and my lifestyle aren't compatible — you know that better than anyone."

"Wait a minute." She stood up, trembling with shocked anger. I never mentioned marriage — and I've never asked you for promises!"

"You never mentioned you were a virgin either," he said harshly. "I'm too old a hand to be trapped by an inexperienced girl who hears wedding bells just because a man takes her to bed."

"But I love you!" she cried fatally.

An emotion she couldn't read touched his eyes and was gone.

"Oh come on Julia, that's the oldest line in the world. You don't know me, let alone love me."

"And last night meant nothing to you?" She remembered his tenderness, his hands gentling her fears. Surely that wasn't merely technique?

"A pleasant memory. Don't be melodramatic Julia, you're making this very difficult for both of us. I've got to go."

As the room came back into focus Julia found her fingers had cramped on the door handle. That whole part of her life was behind her, she wouldn't let him hurt her again.

Ten minutes later she stepped out of the shower listening intently for signs of movement downstairs. Perhaps he'd gone; she'd made it plain enough he wasn't welcome. Then she heard the sharp click of the percolator being switched on — so he'd taken her sarcastic comment about coffee literally. Well, he needn't think he was going to make himself comfortable to drink it.

She pulled on a track suit, her fingers shaking with anger. She needed that fury, needed it to keep at bay all the muddled, vulnerable, loving feelings she had for Jon despite everything.

If only she knew why he had come, what he was thinking. But then she'd never known what was going on in Jon Farrell's mind, had only guessed at the banked fires smouldering behind the steady dark blue eyes.

With Danny you were never in any doubt about how he felt. When he was happy everyone was included in the party; when he was down he made no bones about it — and when he'd said he wanted to marry her, that it was the right thing for them both it was impossible to resist for long.

It was Danny who'd given her a shoulder to cry on after Jon had run out on her. Then when he'd returned to spend a few months at head office they'd seen each other virtually every day and her gratitude soon turned to affection and trust. The only thing he'd never confided in her was why he too wanted a marriage of convenience. He'd convinced her that it would work, they'd be happy together, they'd have the children they both wanted so much. Hopelessly loving Jon would never bring her that family, and Danny seemed to need her as Jon never would.

Julia put her brush down on the dressing-table and automatically checked her appearance in the mirror. There were dark shadows under her eyes, stark against the paleness of her skin. Normally by July she had a healthy golden tan, but not this year. Perhaps Jon had some justification for suspecting her of drinking, she conceded grudgingly.

From half-way down the stairs she could see Jon slumped in the deep armchair sipping coffee, his long legs stretched out. Resentment filled her: how dare he sit there without a care in the world when his very presence had thrown her into turmoil!

"If you've finished your coffee, I suggest you go," she said from the door.

Jon shifted his shoulders, tipping his blond head back on the cushions, calmly ignoring her inhospitality. "I haven't done what I came for."

"Which was?"

Jon put his mug on the hearth and fished in the back pocket of his jeans. "Sir Max asked me to give you this. He wants you to come back to work."

"If Sir Max wants me he's quite capable of ringing me up and telling me so. I can't imagine what he's got in mind — I can hardly expect my old job back — I resigned."

Jon still held out the letter. "Oh, give it to me then."

Julia muttered ungraciously. It was crumpled and warm from his body heat. She tossed it dismissively on to the sideboard. So he'd only come because Sir Max had sent him, not because he'd wanted to see her.

"What's wrong with the post?"

Jon dropped back into the chair and shrugged. "He seemed to think you wouldn't read it." He paused, his eyes mocking her. "I can't imagine why. He told me both he and Lady Faulkner were very worried about you."

"It's a pity you've got nothing better to do than sit around gossiping about me." As soon as it was out Julia knew she was being unfair, at least to Sir Max and his wife.

"I've got plenty to do," Jon snapped

back, goaded at last, "and I could well do without trailing round the Home Counties running Max's errands! I don't give a damn what you decide, just read the letter so I can go back and tell him you've seen it."

Julia scanned it rapidly. She'd intended ringing Sir Max tomorrow; now it would look as if she'd been cajoled back to work for her own good by two paternalistic men!

Sir Max meant well, he'd always been more of an uncle than a boss in the six years she'd worked at Faulkner Engineering. He'd been the one who'd spotted her potential, given her the job in face of criticism she was too young for it. But that didn't give him the right to run her life.

"I don't want special treatment." Jon's mouth quirked in amused disbelief but he said nothing. "And I certainly don't need you acting as messenger boy. Isn't a little beneath you Jon? After all, you didn't even turn up for the funeral."

Jon straightened in the chair, his

mouth tight and defensive. "We'd lost one of our best engineers, someone had to stay and get on with the work."

"And I lost my husband, your best friend." It was a cry of pain from her heart, tears stung the back of her eyes and she turned away quickly before he saw them.

"You didn't want me there — you had your family, Max and Joan, all your friends . . . "

"What about loyalty to Danny?" Julia rounded on him, anger drying her tears. "You were supposed to be his best friend — he never once criticised you, even though I told him how badly you treated me!"

Jon was white under his tan. "That's the way you saw it . . . "

"What other way was there to see it?"

Jon stood up abruptly. "Stop it! Stop winding yourself up into an emotional state."

"How dare you!"

"I expected you to mourn, and I

expected you to act like the intelligent woman you are — which means not shutting yourself up with a bottle of whisky for company." Without waiting for her reaction he sauntered past her into the kitchen asking casually over his shoulder. "Coffee? I'm having another cup."

Shocked by his total lack of sympathy Julia watched as he poured her coffee. This was all wrong, this wasn't how she'd imagined this confrontation with Jon.

Jon handed her the cup then flopped back into his chair.

Julia banged down her cup on the sideboard, the hot liquid splashing the polish. "What's this for?" She gestured at the coffee. "My supposed hangover?"

He shrugged. "If you like. It does work, and you look as if you need it." He bent and tightened the laces on his battered trainers. "Or better still, get out and get some exercise, work it off." He ran a finger through the film of dust on the glass coffee table. "Or you could start by doing some housework."

Julia stalked into the kitchen to find a cloth to mop up the spills. Insufferable man! He was the sloppiest housekeeper she'd ever come across. She reached across the sink for the dishcloth, then recoiled at the overpowering smell of Scotch. Jon had poured her father's ten-year-old malt whisky down the sink. The bottle protruded from the rubbish-bin. Julia snatched it up and stormed back into the living-room.

"I'd like to wrap this round your head, but apart from making me feel a lot better it wouldn't serve any useful purpose." She waved the bottle towards the door. "You can just go down to the off-licence and buy my father another bottle. And deliver it yourself — that way you can tell him what you've done with his birthday present. You ... you think you can stroll back, ordering me about, accusing me of being a drunk ... "

Jon's movement was so swiftly silent

she jumped when his hands touched her shoulders. "Julia I'm sorry . . . I shouldn't have said that — or thought it either." His fingers compelled her face him. For a moment she resisted then gave in.

He was so close she could see the pulse beating at his throat. The last time they'd been this close they'd been in each other's arms, in the big bed upstairs. That was before he'd made his 'we're both adults' speech.

Jon's hands tightened on her shoulders, then he bent and kissed her, his lips warm and hard. Julia wrenched herself free.

"Just what do you want Jon?" she demanded. "To take what you want again then clear off?"

The colour swept back into his face, his eyes were flinty blue chips. "So I took what I wanted did I? I was under the impression we both wanted what happened."

"You took advantage of me — I was in love with you," Julia flared, knowing as she said it how unfair she was being.

"Don't make me sound like some Victorian seducer. You knew exactly what we were doing. I never made you any promises."

"I never asked you for promises!" Julia was shouting now. "Did you think I wanted to trap you into marrying me? All I asked for was honesty — and I didn't get it."

"You knew the job came first . . ."

"It didn't for Danny," Julia hit back.

"Danny had other priorities" Jon's blue eyes held her angry gaze.

"What's that supposed to mean? Just for once can't you say what you mean? How could I ever have trusted you enough to . . ."

"Sacrifice your virginity?" Jon finished for her sardonically. "Making love with me was so repellent was it? Strange, but at the time I thought you were enjoying it. Go on, I'm waiting to hear you deny it," he persisted.

"I can't deny it," she choked out.

"You . . . you bring out the worst in me! Danny . . . "

"If only you knew the truth about your Danny . . . " He checked himself with an obvious effort.

"Get out! Get out and don't come back!"

The living-room door slammed, the noise echoing through the empty house. Julia sank into the nearest chair. She'd seen him again, been in his arms and had kept her love for him hidden. That was what she wanted, wasn't it? So why did she feel so awful?

2

"**D**AMN and blast!" When her gardener trimmed the lawn edges they followed a smooth curve: now they looked like they'd been cut out with pinking shears.

"Stop massacring that lawn, I can't bear it," her sister's amused voice said from the french windows.

Julia dropped the trimmers into the flowerbed. "Meg! Don't creep up on me like that!" She threw her arms round her elder sister and gave her a big hug. "What are you doing here? I wasn't expecting you."

"I thought you were still on holiday, but when I drove past and saw the front door open . . ."

A vivid picture of Jon's angry departure came into Julia's mind. "My last visitor must have forgotten to shut it behind him."

27

"He?" Meg's dark brows quirked. "Sounds interesting."

"Not interesting — aggravating. But never mind that, can you stay for lunch? It's ages since I've seen you."

"Sorry, but I've been rushed off my feet. I'm in danger of becoming successful. It's really quite worrying; I may be making some money at last!"

Julia smiled affectionately at her elegant sister as she curled up on a garden seat.

Meg's hand-painted silk clothes had always sold, but a buyer from a top London store had recently promised to take everything she could turn out.

Meg looked at the castellated edges of the lawn. "Would you like a hand?"

"I've finished, but I still ought to do something with the roses." Julia hacked at a drooping bloom.

"Whose head is that you're chopping off?"

"Jon Farrell's," Julia said without thinking.

"Your last visitor?"

28

"Got it in one." Julia threw down her secateurs. "Come on, let's have a glass of lemon tea and I'll tell you all about it."

Meg cast a critical eye round the kitchen as they waited for the kettle to boil. "Place looks a bit of a mess."

"Don't you start, I've had it all from Mr Farrell this morning, lecturing me on 'not letting myself go' and 'the dangers of alcohol' and 'the benefits of getting back to work'."

"So the gorgeous Jon's back in your life — lucky you."

"Gorgeous! He's rude, opinionated, overbearing, sexist . . . "

"Shame you're in love with him then," Meg said slyly.

"How did you know? Is it that obvious?"

"Only to me. I could never understand how, loving Jon as you do, you married Danny. How was the visit by the way?"

"Grim. They're all still so upset. I felt an awful fraud Meg, so hypocritical . . . of

29

course I miss Danny . . . "

"I would have thought if anyone would understand a marriage of convenience it would be Danny's family," Meg commented, unknowingly echoing Danny's argument.

"You guessed then?"

"Of course I did! One minute you're on cloud nine, in love with Jon, then six months later you're married to Danny." She picked up the cups and carried them through to the living-room.

"What happened?"

"I didn't mean to fall in love with Jon. When I first started going out with him he was just another attractive engineer in England for a couple of months. We had a lot in common, same sense of humour, same way of seeing things. All very friendly, he hardly laid a finger on me."

"And then?"

"He kissed me." Julia's mouth softened in a reminiscent smile. "The whole fairy-tale bit: bells rang, stars came out . . . I'd never felt like that for anyone before. I realised I loved him, thought it was the same for him too. My mistake. After we made love he made it clear it was very nice so far as it went — but he didn't love me, he didn't want commitment. He didn't even want to see me again."

"So you married Danny on the rebound? That doesn't sound like you."

"No, it wasn't that. Danny said he realised I would never love anyone the way I loved Jon but that was OK by him. He couldn't marry for love either, but he wanted a wife, a home a family. It seemed like a sensible arrangement. I loved him as much as anyone who wasn't Jon, but it was a different thing — friendship, trust . . . " Seeing the disbelief in her sister's eyes she insisted. "It *would* have worked!"

"What was in it for Danny? How could he be so certain it was right for him?"

"It was the only thing he wouldn't

31

tell me. I believed he wanted to marry me, but he never told me why. It sounds so crazy now, but at the time it seemed the right thing to do."

"And now?"

"Now I need to get back to work. I'm going back to Faulkner's."

"Is that why Jon was here?"

"Yes, as Sir Max's errand boy. The pair of them think it would be good for me to get back to work."

"How galling, now it will look as if you're only going back because they've persuaded you." Meg gazed into her empty teacup. "How do you feel about working with Jon again?"

"I won't be. He'll be off again in a week or two — or I'll be looking for another job, believe me!"

"Why so hostile? You've admitted you still love him. You're both older and wiser — try again."

"Oh no." Julia said bitterly, "he made his feelings very clear. He'd never have come near me if Sir Max hadn't sent him — mind you that didn't stop him trying it on . . . "

"He kissed you?" Meg sat up in her chair.

"Yes, and goodness knows where it would have ended if I'd gone along with him. Bells, stars all over again for me, and just another affair for him — but I'm not prepared to settle for that, not with *anyone* and especially not with someone I love."

★ ★ ★

On Monday Julia phoned Faulkner's and was put through to Sir Max's office so swiftly it was obvious they were expecting her call.

"Julia, glad you rang. I gather you'd already made the decision to come back. Come to lunch today and we'll thrash out the details."

She would have to get a move on. Julia slipped off her dressing-gown and had a rapid shower then slid back the mirrored doors of the wardrobe in search for something suitable for the

33

July heat. She selected a linen dress in a cool moss green that flattered her eyes.

Outside the front door Julia put on her sunglasses, turned the key in the lock and stood savouring the moment. This was it, she was about to start living her own life again.

There was a white Golf GTi parked in the space marked 'Personnel Officer'. Julia's mouth twisted in a wry smile at herself as she manoeuvered Danny's BMW into another parking spot. She'd resigned as personnel officer and until she spoke to Max she wasn't sure what her status within the company would be.

In the lift travelling to the third floor Julia felt as it she'd never been away, as if today were a normal working day and her appointment with Sir Max no more than a routine meeting.

Sally, Sir Max's PA was welcoming as she looked up from her word processor. With a grin she pressed the button on the intercom. "Mrs Leyton's here sir."

Max Faulkner scowled up at Julia from a mass of technical drawings which spilled off the desk on to the carpet. She was used to this sort of reception, knew her old boss well enough to recognise the affection behind the scowl.

"You meant it then, good, we need you." He punched the button on his intercom and yelled, "Sally! Get this junk off my desk. Sit down Julia."

Sally, scooped up the rolls of drawings and, her back to Sir Max, pulled a wry face at Julia.

"Go and get your lunch now Sally. Julia and I will be lunching upstairs and I don't want any interruptions."

He waited until the door closed behind her then said, "You look good. How do you feel?"

"I know I'm ready to come back," she stated quietly. "You didn't need to send Jon Farrell."

"Mm, with hindsight that was probably a mistake — he was none too keen to do it anyway. Let's go up to lunch and I'll fill you in on what's been happening in your department."

Julia followed Sir Max to the lift. So Jon hadn't wanted to come and see her! Involuntarily, her fingers strayed to her lips, feeling again the pressure of his firm mouth on hers.

As Max pushed open the door to the directors' dining-room Julia pushed all thoughts of Jon Farrell to the back of her mind: there were more important things to concentrate on now.

It was the first time she'd eaten in this room. The food was laid out as a cold buffet with mineral water and fruit juice at the end. Julia's lips quirked, archetypal Max — there was nothing to encourage lengthy, boozy lunches here.

"So, who's been running Personnel since I left? Anyone I know?"

Max Faulkner buttered a roll. "Drew Scott."

"Drew Scott?" Julia echoed. "But wasn't he in Export?" She was surprised, and showed it. Drew was a good manager but he's had no experience in Personnel.

"Yes but he's wasted there. He's got the capacity to go a lot further; I want him to get experience in all departments. A short spell in Personnel is a good jumping-off point. If he's got a fault it's seeing the job solely in terms of cash flow. He needed to learn that this business is about people too."

Julia looked at the wily old fox opposite her. What was he up to? She remembered Drew Scott — what woman wouldn't! Tall, dark and handsome summed him up perfectly. Miraculously, he was also efficient, intelligent and a thoroughly nice person. Was Sir Max grooming him as his successor?

In ten years' time her boss would be seventy and Drew Scott would be forty-five. Just right to take over one of the premier engineering companies in the country.

"You go ahead, don't wait for me," Sir Max said. Julia helped herself to a chicken salad and a glass of Perrier water. Returning to the table she was suddenly struck by how alike Max and Jon were. Not in looks or in manner, but in a shared intangible toughness and self-reliance, and restlessness.

She remembered the office gossip in the months before she'd married Danny, the rumours that Jon was the Old Man's chosen successor. If that position was now threatened by Scott, Jon was in for a nasty shock. Julia wondered if he knew.

Faulkner came back to the table. "Scott's done a reasonable holding job but he hadn't got your flair with people. I've been holding that job for you Julia. Can you start Monday?"

Julia was stunned. "But I resigned!"

"I was prepared to give it six months, then if you were still sitting at home I'd have replaced you."

"I accept — and thank you for your faith in me," Julia managed to say.

"Don't think I've gone soft. If you hadn't been damn good at your job I'd have washed my hands of you." That sounded more like the Max Faulkner she knew and loved!

"There's one thing though — I can't just walk back and take over cold. Can you spare Drew for a week or so?"

"Just what I was going to suggest. I'll give you a fortnight together, but knowing you, I suspect you'll need less."

Over dessert he filled her in about the company's latest projects and the major staff changes. "And there's something else," he added, lowering his voice, although the room was emptying fast, "there's something big coming up in the next month. I can't say any more just yet until it's been ratified by the Board, so keep it under your hat, but get your desk clear — your department's going to be heavily involved."

Julia raised her eyebrows. "Sounds intriguing. I'll make sure I'm up to date by then."

Sir Max pushed back his chair, tossing his napkin on to the table. "Knowing you Julia I don't doubt it. Let's go down and see Scott: he's expecting you."

Her boss left her outside the familiar door marked Personnel Department. "I'll leave you two to sort things out between you. See you next Monday." He set off down the corridor, then turned. "Oh, and by the way Julia — it's good to have you back."

Buoyed up by this unexpected show of sentiment she pushed open the door into the secretary's office. A small plump girl jumped to her feet, rushing to throw her arms round Julia. "Mrs Leyton, you're back. Great!"

Julia disentangled herself gently, smiling into Angela's face. It's good to be back," she responded.

A masculine voice behind her said, "Come on Angela — I've not been that bad to work for have I?" Drew Scott leaned against the door-frame of the inner office.

Predictably Angela blushed; Julia remembered him having this effect on all the secretaries. Impeccably dressed as always in a black suit and a shirt of startling whiteness Drew stepped forward and offered Julia his hand. "Welcome back Mrs Leyton. Excuse me a moment, I'll be right back."

Startled, Julia noticed he was holding a large screwdriver and a metal plaque. With a flourish he screwed it to the outer office door. "There you are," he gestured to her reinstated nameplate, "restored to your rightful place."

Her office was virtually unchanged. It was a large room, light and airy, her desk near the window and a small group of deep armchairs at one end, the place where she sat down face to face with staff when they came to her with a problem. The only addition was a second desk, at right-angles to her own.

"Hope that's OK with you Mrs Leyton, it seemed the best place to put it while we're working together." He dropped the screwdriver into a drawer. "Shall we ask Angela to bring in some coffee?"

"That's up to you," Julia laughed, "this is all yours until Monday, you make the difficult executive decisions! And call me Julia, please."

Drew chuckled. "Right, in that case, for two please Angela."

They sat down in the armchairs. Drew produced a slim manilla file, tossing it on to the low table between them. "I've put these notes together for you; you might find it useful to go over them before Monday."

Julia picked up the file, thumbing through quickly. Drew had summarised the company's current projects, listed all the staff changes and added some notes of his own.

"This will be invaluable, Drew, thank you. How on earth did you get it together so quickly? I've only just confirmed things with Sir Max."

"Jon Farrell stopped by first thing and told me you were coming back." He seemed puzzled by her surprise. "I realised it wasn't official but I knew he'd just come from the Boss."

What was Jon playing at, thought Julia furiously. He could have made her working relationship with Drew impossible. Or perhaps that was the general idea. Sir Max had said Jon hadn't wanted to see her, or to persuade her to come back. It seemed he didn't want her at Faulkner Engineering at all!

"He'd absolutely no right to tell you. I'm sorry Drew, you shouldn't have heard it that way — I hadn't even properly made up my mind." Drew Scott was looking politely non-committal; Julia felt she had to give him some explanation. "Jon Farrell called round uninvited yesterday. He made me so cross I blurted out my plans to come back before I'd finalised things with the Boss!"

"Don't worry, I'm not offended, I knew you'd be back soon. I was more than happy to sit in for you; it's been interesting and useful experience — but I won't pretend I've been doing more than caretaking." He smiled ruefully. "Everyone's been very tolerant, but I've lost count of the times I've been asked when you'd be back."

She could have kicked herself for being so indiscreet — and so unprofessional. The last thing a personnel manager should do is to express a personal opinion about one member of staff to another — especially when the two were potential rivals.

Drew closed the office door. "What's the problem between you two?"

"He was my husband's friend, not mine," Julia replied cautiously. She was shocked that Jon was making no attempt to hide the way he felt. Sir Max had commented on it, now Drew. It hurt — and it was so unjust. She'd done nothing to hurt him, she wasn't the one who'd walked out . . .

Drew was watching her intently. "Perhaps he blames you for splitting up their partnership." He broke off in some confusion, "I mean, before Danny was killed . . . oh hell! Shall we just forget I said that?"

"It's OK, I don't mind talking

about Danny." Then the implication hit her. "What do you mean about them splitting up?"

"Jon wasn't leaving the Company as well was he?" Drew looked as confused as she felt.

"Leaving!" She stared at him bemused. "What are you talking about? Danny had no plans to leave Faulkner's."

"I'm sorry." Drew looked appalled. "I assumed you knew . . . "

Julia was suddenly cold. "I didn't know. I want to see his resignation." She stood up, the filing — cabinet keys in her hand.

Drew rose swiftly, "Look, I don't think this is such a good idea. You've had a shock. Sit down and I'll get Angela to bring the coffee through. We'll talk about this later . . . "

"I don't want coffee," Julia contradicted flatly. "I want to see that letter now. Something's going on that I didn't know about and I want to find out just what it is!"

Danny's characteristic sprawled signature was unmistakable. "Singapore! And I've never heard of this company!" Bewildered, she held out the letter to Drew.

"I have," he said. "They're American bridge specialists. They don't do much in the UK or Europe but they've cornered the market in the Far East."

Julia sank down in the chair, reading and re-reading the letter as though it contained some clue to Danny's inexplicable behaviour. Why hadn't he told her? He wrote twice a week, told her everything — or so she'd believed. How could he keep a change as major as this, as crucial to their carefully arranged life together, a secret?

The black type blurred, then leapt into focus as she read the date — the 19th — the day Danny was killed.

"Are you OK Julia?" Drew was on his knees beside her, his arm round her shoulders. She hadn't even noticed.

"Danny wrote this the day he was killed. He wrote to me as well, but

I've never opened the letter. I couldn't bear to." Suddenly there were tears in her eyes. "That's why I didn't know. It's my fault I didn't know. I must go home and open the letter. I'll see you Monday morning Drew."

In the car on the way home Julia thought hard about Danny, about his taking another job without even consulting her. A change like that wasn't a spur of the moment decision. He must have been through at least two interviews. Had he told Jon?

The unsettling thought grew that she'd known less about her husband than she'd thought she had. Why had he felt unable to tell her? Whatever their unconventional marriage had been it had been based on frankness. She'd always known there was something in his past he hadn't told her, but their agreement had been that they'd share everything in the future.

The letters were in the hall-table where she'd stuffed them when Jon had arrived the day before. The others spilled to the floor as she ripped open the last envelope and began to read.

. . . so it's been a pretty boring week, absolutely no news. Its hotter than ever — if that's possible. The biggest excitement for days was Jon finding a scorpion in the bath — I don't know who was more put out, Jon or the scorpion!
I miss you, only two more months to go and I'll be home again.
Love, Danny

She rechecked the envelope to see if she'd missed a sheet of the flimsy airmail paper, a note included at the last moment, but there was nothing.

Julia sat down on the bottom stair and began to re-read the letters. An hour later the last sheet joined the drift of paper at her feet. She'd searched for a clue why Danny had made a major a career change without giving her the slightest hint. She hadn't found it — and it had left her more worried and confused than if she had.

Julia twisted the diamond engagement ring on her left hand. Danny had been open, honest, quite incapable of keeping a secret. Presents were always days early because he could never keep a surprise to himself. It was inconceivable he could keep quiet about something as major as this.

The only explanation she could think of was he was planning to break the good news to her on his next leave. He wouldn't move from Faulkner's unless he'd been tempted by a very good offer — he'd want to celebrate. Knowing Danny, he'd have booked a weekend in Paris at the very least!

Stiffly, she got to her feet and carried the letters through to the living-room grate. She dropped them on the ashes and struck a match. As the smoke curled up the chimney she watched the flames uneasily, unconvinced in her heart by her own explanation of his silence.

Had he offered to marry her out

of misplaced chivalry, realised too late what he'd committed himself to? Knowing how badly she'd been hurt by Jon he'd have done anything not to hurt her again, even change jobs to put a greater geographical distance between them so she'd have less opportunity to realise something had gone wrong.

Whatever the explanation she had to be sure she hadn't been selfish in agreeing to marry Danny. Julia knew her conscience wouldn't let her rest until she got to the bottom of this. And the only person who might know was Jon. However she felt about him she had to go and see him, find out what Jon had meant when he'd jibed, "If only you knew the truth about your Danny."

3

"CAN I help you, Miss?"
"I'm looking for Mr Farrell. Which is his boat?" The breeze from the river was unexpectedly cool. Julia reached into the car for the jacket of her suede trouser suit, slammed the door and locked it.

"He went off in his car about an hour ago. Gone shopping I expect, he usually does on Saturday mornings," the man added knowledgeably.

"Oh . . . " deflated, Julia turned back to the car. It had taken her a long time to work out how to approach Jon without betraying the truth about her marriage. He must never guess she'd married Danny for anything but love. She'd keyed herself up to face him, and now he wasn't here she'd have to go through it all again.

"He won't be long though. The

man consulted his watch. "Another half hour or so at the most. You a friend of his?" He came a little closer, his eyes running over her slender figure in the russet-red trousers and cream camisole top.

"You seem to know a lot about his movements," she commented coolly.

"It's my job," he shrugged. "Got to keep an eye on the boats haven't I? Know who's coming and going. You can come and wait in my office if you like, have a nice cup of coffee."

"I don't think so. Just show me Mr Farrell's boat, I'll wait there."

"Suit yourself. Third boat down, the big one with the blue paint."

Julia turned her back on him with a nod of acknowledgment and picked her way across the mooring ropes along the bank. The first boat was shrouded in heavy covers, the second, a big motor cruiser, shone like a new pin with gleaming brasswork and fresh paint. The owner stood on deck, a jaunty yachting cap pushed to the back of his head, a tin of Brasso in one hand.

"Good morning," he called pleasantly. "Looking for someone?"

"Jon Farrell," Julia smiled back. "I gather he's out shopping so I'll wait."

The man gave her a mock salute and settled into his deckchair with the Financial Times. Julia suppressed a giggle. He was precisely her idea of a retired bank manager.

Gingerly Julia stepped onto the short gangplank sloping down to the unvarnished deck at the stern. She'd thought to put on flat, rubber soled shoes instead of heels, but one glance round the boat told her she needn't have worried. However Jon spent his time, it wasn't polishing the deck — or the brasswork.

Stooping, she looked through the dusty windows, but the curtains were closed on the bank side. She worked her way round the narrow gangway to the front of the boat, but all the curtains in the front cabin were drawn. She'd never been on board the boat he'd bought when he'd moved out of Danny's house after their engagement. Only her overwhelming need to find out about Danny had brought her here. Now she was beginning to have doubts about the wisdom of coming. The sudden splash of oars startled her as a rowing eight swept past intent on their rhythmic stroke, the cox yelling shrill orders. It was all so very English: the sun dappled willows, the man on the next boat polishing his brass. How could she talk to Jon, here or anywhere else? He was the last person she could discuss her marriage with.

Coming here, on his territory, was a mistake. She'd write a note asking him to call and see her, slide it under the cabin door and go. Julia tore a page out of her Filofax and scribbled a brief message then steadied herself on the handle as she crouched to push the scrap of paper under the varnished door. With a click it swung open and after a moment's hesitation she stepped into the gloom of the saloon which occupied half the cabin space.

She'd just leave the note on the bureau and go. Jon would know she'd been there, but he'd find out anyway from the neighbours.

In the half light she caught her foot on the edge of the rug, and stumbled. This was ridiculous! Fumbling about like a thief in the night! She'd just as much right to walk uninvited into his home as he had into hers. She opened the chintz curtains, letting the sunlight flood into the long room, revealing the spartan furnishings. Only the piles of books on the shelves under the windows spoke of Jon.

Julia could never resist books. She crossed and began to read the titles, her head tilted to one side, a curtain of dark hair falling over one shoulder. Several of the titles were in Arabic, a text on falconry, an English-Arabic dictionary. Julia picked up a copy of the poems of Omar Khayyam.

Poetry! Somehow she'd never imagined Jon reading poetry, yet the limp red cover was dog-eared with use. Julia flicked through and began to read aloud.

"*Here with a loaf of bread beneath the bough,*

A flask of wine . . ."

From behind her Jon's voice softly completed the lines:

"*. . . a book of verse — and thou.* How appropriate."

Julia spun round to face him, her heart thudding in surprise at his cat-like approach. "I didn't hear you come in," she began, furious at the way her heart beat at the sight of him.

"So I see," Jon remarked laconically. He was dressed in blue jeans and an oversize white sweatshirt which emphasised his deep tan. He was carrying a large brown paper sack of groceries, but the effect was far from domesticated. He looked sexy — and dangerous.

Julia breathed deeply, fighting the frightening wave of feeling that hit her. Desire — that was all it was she tried to tell herself. It was all it had ever been for him, and stupidly she'd mistaken it for love. Ignore it, she told herself fiercely.

"I can't offer you a flask of wine," he called from the galley. Abruptly Julia pulled herself together. She'd been so taken aback she hadn't realised he'd moved. She could hear cupboard doors opening and shutting as he put the groceries away. "Will a cup of coffee do?"

Why not? She was here now — and so was he. She may as well stick to her original plan however rattled she was feeling.

"Yes please." She joined him in the tiny galley. "I came to talk to you. You left the door open, so I thought I'd come in and write a note." She held out the piece of paper.

Jon leaned back against the counter, long legs crossed at the ankles. He took the note from her but made no move to read it. Despite all her resolution to be cool Julia fidgeted under his steady regard. None of his feelings about finding her on his boat showed. All Julia could discern was a faint quizzical twist of his lips.

"Well, read it!"

His brown fingers with their short, oval nails toyed with the folded paper, teasing her. "Now let's see . . . it's not my birthday, or payday . . . and you're looking far too gorgeous for it to be anything nasty . . . " There was laughter in his voice now, and warmth in his eyes. The old Jon, the one she hadn't seen for so long, was back as though their parting was a half-remembered nightmare. Suddenly he was dangerously close in the confines of the tiny galley.

Julia took a step back, away from the ridiculous temptation to walk into his arms. Jon seemed to sense her unease, stopped teasing her and read the few scribbled lines.

"So, what do you want to talk to me about?"

Now it had come to the point the

right words wouldn't come. How on earth could she ask him about Danny without admitting something about the true state of her marriage?

"Julia?" Jon touched her shoulder lightly. "What's the matter?" She stiffened at his touch, the warmth of his fingers on her bare skin, then saw him register her reaction. His eyes narrowed and he dropped his hand abruptly. "What do you want to ask me about?" he repeated.

"About Danny."

"Oh . . . " he said flatly, turning to plug in the kettle.

Julia tugged sharply at his sleeve forcing him to turn and face her. In the narrow galley their bodies were almost touching, his tension palpable. She was positive he was hiding something from her.

"Jon I want to know what you were implying about Danny the other day," she said levelly.

The hard features relaxed, the deep blue gaze clearing. "Nothing, you made me lose my temper, that's all."

It wasn't true and she knew it, but it was no good tackling him head on. He lifted the jug to pour coffee and she saw the whiteness of his knuckles as he gripped it. She realised he was angry. But why — and at whom?

Julia picked up her cup and walked through into the saloon, curling up on one of the wide window seats. Jon was on his guard now; she'd have to try other tactics if she was to achieve what she'd come for.

"Were you thinking of leaving Faulkner's too?"

"Too?" He stopped dead in the doorway, his eyes wary.

Julia sipped her coffee, watching him as he sat in the swivel chair at the bureau. He was keeping his distance, physically and mentally. She hadn't expected so much resistance. Why was he putting up these barriers?

"Well with Danny taking that Far East job, and Sir Max grooming Drew Scott as his successor . . . I'd have

60

thought you'd want out."

How did you find out about Danny's plans to leave Faulkner's?" He sat up sharply, then relaxed. "Ah yes, your little foray into the Personnel Department yesterday . . . did Max tell you — or the ubiquitous Mr Scott?"

So he knew that Danny hadn't told her. She wasn't prepared for how much that hurt. What else had Danny told his friend that he hadn't told his wife?

Instinctively she hit back. "So it's true what they say — you are jealous of Drew Scott."

Jon gave a great shout of laughter, his untrimmed mane of blond hair thrown back, broad shoulders shaking with mirth. Of all the reactions she'd expected, hoped for, it wasn't this.

"Drew Scott!" he gasped finally. "That man's no threat to anything that's important to me."

If the company wasn't important to him, what was? Could it be that the death of his best friend had robbed him of his motivation. Suddenly Julia felt ashamed of her cheap jibe.

"Jon . . . I'm sorry I was such a bitch. I should have realised . . . I lost a husband, but you a close friend too." She crossed to where he sat and tentatively touched his. shoulder. "I should have thought of that before I opened my mouth."

Jon's hand covered hers, his fingers warm and sure. For a moment she was certain he was going to say something about Danny, but his mouth relaxed into a smile. "Forget it Julia. Stay for lunch." He squeezed her fingers briefly, then stood up, stretching as if throwing off a burden. "Let's eat on deck, enjoy the sunshine."

Julia hesitated, torn between the need to find out about Danny and apprehension at being alone with Jon. It was a painful luxury being here with him, loving him as she did, aching to tell him, touch him, but having to guard every word and gesture.

"Or had you something else planned this afternoon?"

"Such as?" she queried. "The last few months I've spent pretty much alone. People avoid you when you've been widowed."

"You'll be fine once you get back to work." Jon moved around the deck as he spoke, setting up chairs and a folding table. "You're not having second thoughts about coming back are you?" He paused, tablecloth in one hand and scrutinised her face. "Does Scott resent you displacing him?" Jon's tone made it clear he wouldn't put it past him to do so.

Julia took the cloth from him and spread it over the table. "There's no love lost between you and Drew, is there?"

Jon's eyes narrowed at the implied familiarity in her use of the christian name. "Tut, tut, very unprofessional of you to try to discuss one member of the senior staff with another!"

Suddenly the tension between them had gone, replaced by something that was almost friendship. Julia stuck out her tongue at him. "I'm not back at work yet — I can be as indiscreet as I like until Monday. Anyway, you brought it up."

"So I did."

"You haven't answered my question. Why don't you like Drew?" she persisted.

Jon shrugged. "He's like a thousand other competent managers, and that's fine as far as it goes. But he's not an engineer — and that's what Faulkner's is all about."

"You're being unreasonable Jon — everyone who works for the firm doesn't have to be an engineer. I'm not!"

"Ah, but you're not aiming to be our next Managing Director are you?" He went back inside the saloon, stooping under the low doorway. "Bread and cheese and salad OK? What do you want to drink? I've got lager, orange juice, Perrier . . ."

"Not lager," she called back. "Perrier and orange will be fine. Can I help?"

"Nope." He dumped down an armful of bottles. "I'll put everything on the table and we can help ourselves. This isn't the Ritz."

"How true." Julia looked round at the dusty deck and peeling paintwork. "And you had the nerve to criticise *my* housework."

Jon sat down and began to cut a French loaf ignoring her jibe. Innocently she looked at him, her hazed eyes wide, and remarked, "And why do you assume I'm not in the running for Managing Director? It could be my life-long ambition . . . you could be making a mistake if you think Drew Scott's the only threat to your plans."

"Is this business about Scott mere speculation — or has Max said something? Cheddar or Brie?" Under the lightness of his voice Julia sensed a consuming need to know.

"Brie please. Max did just happen to mention something of his plans for the future over lunch yesterday. But of course, it was all off the record." Julia smiled sweetly at him and sipped her drink.

"Don't play games Julia," he was suddenly serious. "If Max had anything to say about me I want to know what it was."

Instantly Julia was sorry she'd teased him with the subject. "He didn't mention you Jon, honestly. He just said something about putting Drew in Personnel to give him more experience."

"Forget I mentioned it," his voice was brusque.

Oh damn! Julia thought. This was no way to get him to open up and talk about Danny. The shuttered look was in his eyes as he sipped his lager.

Needling him kept him at a safe distance but it was totally counter-productive: she would never find the truth about Danny if there was this constant antagonism between them. And instead of making her feel better, she just felt a bitch.

They finished lunch in silence. Julia scraped back her chair, picked up her bag and jacket and stood up, unsure of what to say in farewell.

"Going?" Jon looked surprised to find her on her feet. He'd obviously been in a world of his own.

"I think it would be best. Goodbye Jon." She turned, one foot on the gangplank.

"But you can't go!" he protested with such feeling Julia's heart leapt in response.

She came back and faced him across the littered table. "Why not?"

"You haven't done the washing up." He grinned, the sudden flash of white teeth transforming his face.

Julia snatched up the heel of the French bread and threw it at his head. "You . . . you asked me to lunch — do your own washing up!"

Jon ducked, the bread splashed into the water and was eagerly gulped down by a passing swan. "The choice is yours — wash up or make the coffee."

"I'll make the coffee. You can wash up."

She was at the minute sink filling the kettle as he came in with the plates, heard him pause in the galley doorway, knew he was watching her as she leaned over the sink. The skin on the nape of her neck prickled under the intensity of his look. Her hair had fallen in a heavy sweep to one side; self-consciously she pushed it back over the exposed skin.

Carefully Jon put down the plates and reached out to run his index finger lightly down the curve of her shoulder to the thin strap of the camisole. At the touch Julia stiffened, then turned off the tap and plugged in the kettle, trying to act as if nothing was happening. Jon let his hand rest lightly on the silky skin feeling her tension as she kept her head averted.

The moment stretched on, then she whispered, "Jon don't . . . please."

He turned her round to face him, both hands cupping her shoulders.

"Don't what Julia? Don't touch you?" His voice was compelling. "What are you so afraid of? Of wanting me as

68

much as I want you?"

He'd finally put it into words, the truth about what he'd always felt about her: wanting, not loving. Unwillingly Julia met his challenging dark gaze.

"Yes I want you," she said levelly. The words were cool but they were what he wanted to hear and it showed in his eyes.

"Julia . . . " His voice was husky.

"No Jon!" She pulled back against his hands. "Listen to me! I admit it — there's a physical attraction, something I can't help . . . but it's not love, although for a while I believed it was — and it's not enough to base a relationship on, I learned that with Danny." Perhaps if she repeated it often enough she'd believe it herself.

Jon's hands dropped to his sides, his face blank. "Danny . . . " He stopped, took a deep breath and began again. "Julia, you can't love a ghost. Danny's dead. Why don't we just take what's here and now? Get on with living.

With deliberate provocation he reached

out and twined his fingers into the hair curling at the nape of her neck. Julia felt his breath falter then his arms encircled her, drawing her close.

"It works Julia, as automatic as pressing a button. We touch — and our bodies take over. It's wonderful — why fight it?"

Nothing had changed. He was still offering her no more of himself than a casual, physical relationship. She'd been a fool to come here, to let things get this far. In a few hours' time she'd be bitterly regretting this, but the knowledge wasn't enough to get her out of his arms, off the boat and safe.

"If you're still in love with Danny I'll settle for what you're offering." Suddenly he was mocking her. "Don't knock it Julia, you know we're good together."

Jon put his fingers under her chin, tipping up her face to take possession of her lips with his. With his touch every sensation became magnified; Julia was startlingly aware of his crisp hair entangled in her fingers, although she wasn't conscious of raising her arms to his neck.

A final flicker of common sense burned in her brain telling her how bitterly she'd regret this afterwards. Then rational thought drowned in sensation as he lifted her in his arms and carried her into his cabin.

Afterwards, she thought, when the fever had passed, he'd understand how empty their lovemaking had been, how little they had to share when their mutual appetite for each other was sated, and he'd leave her, leave her in peace.

But now her hunger for him was a craving, all consuming. His kiss was calculated to send her senses swirling. Even as she responded, matching passion with passion, a tinge of regret lingered that it should have to be like this.

The splash of oars and muffled shouting jolted them both into the

71

real world. There was a bump as something collided with the houseboat. Jon swung round with an oath, leaving her staggering.

"Bloody rowers!"

He yanked the curtains together across the window overlooking the river.

"No one could see in, could they?" Julia asked. She sank on to the end of the bed, vibrating with reaction.

"It's OK, you can only see in from the bank side. Jon turned, gesturing towards the windows and as he did so knocked flying a pile of papers stacked precariously on the chair. Underneath was a battered black attache case marked with the initials DSL.

"That's Danny's case," Julia said, puzzled. "What are you doing with it?" She raised her eyes to his face and saw the shutters come down: he was hiding something from her. "Give it to me!"

"I can't do that Julia," Jon replied levelly. "Everything in it concerns confidential contracts. You can have the case back when I've finished with it."

"I want it now!" She was on her feet grabbing for the handle, but Jon hoisted it easily out of her reach. "If it's so confidential, why have you taken it from the building?" she demanded, suddenly coldly logical. "You know the rules as well as I do. Or doesn't Max know you've got it?"

"Sir Max doesn't know it exists. And we'd better keep it that way until I get a few things sorted out."

"Don't implicate me in whatever you're up to!" she flashed at him furiously. "And don't think I won't tell Sir Max about this."

"I wouldn't push it," he cautioned, his eyes stony.

"Don't threaten me."

"You're not using your head Julia. I warn you — don't make trouble between me and Max. I won't be the loser."

Abruptly Julia spun on her heel and strode to the door. She paused on the threshold and glanced back. "I never want to speak to you again Jon Farrell. The sooner you get sent back to the Middle East the better."

His mocking voice followed her as fled through the saloon. "You're not going to get rid of me so easily Julia . . ."

4

DREW'S Scott's car was parked in the next bay down leaving the space marked 'Personnel Manager' vacant. It was a small thing, like putting back her nameplate, but it pleased Julia.

She swung her legs out of the BMW, smoothing down the soft pleats of her emerald green cotton skirt and adjusting the black leather sash at her waist. It had taken her a long time to decide what to wear on her first day back telling herself it was important to look good on Monday, but knowing in her heart the reason she was keeping busy was Jon.

Saturday had been such a mess! Julia slammed the car door as she thought about it. For a time it had seemed they could be together as friends, but she'd been deluding herself. Jon didn't want a relationship on those terms. Fortunately the real world had intervened in the shape of those inept rowers, saved her from the pain of Jon's reaction a second time. Who knows, in the turmoil of their lovemaking she could have blurted out the truth — that she loved him, had never stopped loving him. Never would.

As for the reasons Jon might have for keeping the briefcase, she pushed them to the back of her mind until she had the emotional energy to think about them. Probably, she told herself sensibly, it was nothing more sinister than Jon wanting to exploit some of Danny's personal contacts, score points against Drew Scott in their competition to be Sir Max's successor.

Drew was already at his desk flicking through the post Angela had just handed him.

"Welcome back!" He was on his feet immediately, coming round the desk to greet her. "Just to make you feel properly at home we've got a bumper bundle of problems in the mail this morning!"

Julia dropped her briefcase beside her chair and smiled back. "Are you sure you haven't been storing them all up for me?"

"As if I would! But seriously, there's a couple of quite tricky problems we'll need to look at first."

"A typical Monday in fact." Julia hung up her jacket and looked round. "Where's Angela? I need a good strong cup of coffee — I'd forgotten how hairy the traffic was at this time in the morning."

Angela came in with a small jug of white rosebuds which she placed with great care on Julia's desk. "Good morning Mrs Leyton."

"Angela — how lovely! Thank you, but you shouldn't have."

"You're right — I shouldn't!" Angela grinned mischievously, looking sideways at Drew Scott. "I pinched them from the Directors' garden on my way up!"

Julia tried to look disapproving, but

failed. "I like a secretary who shows initiative," Drew remarked blandly. "Can you bring us some coffee please?"

Taking a deep breath Julia pulled out the chair and sat down at her desk for the first time in six months. Its tidiness was unnerving.

"It's amazing how disconcerting an empty in-tray is," she commented, making light of her apprehension.

"I'll soon fix that." Drew passed over a folder. "You'll have picked up from those briefing notes I gave you that our biggest headache at the moment is the political situation in the Sudan. There are too many married men on that power plant project for my liking — and that adds up to an awful lot of anxious families at home."

"I saw the report in *The Times* this morning," Julia responded thoughtfully. "We'd better draw up contingency plans in case we need to get them out in a hurry. It won't be the first time I've had to do it."

"Can you bring in the file on the

Central American road project please?"
she asked as Angela came back with the
coffee.

"The one where we had to organise
an airlift?" the secretary queried.

Julia nodded and turned to Drew, "I
hope it won't come to it, but if it does
at least we'll be prepared."

They were soon engrossed in the
problem of drawing up emergency
plans. It was as though she'd never
been away. Julia savoured the stimulus,
the enormous relief of discovering she
was still good at her job. Working with
Drew was an unexpected bonus; at last
she had someone to bounce ideas off,
someone who understood the pressures
of the job.

She'd never really been able to
discuss her work with Danny. Once
or twice she'd got the impression
he thought all the office staff at
Faulkner's had it easy compared to
the field engineers like him and Jon.

"Julia?" Drew prompted, jerking her
out of her distraction.

"Oh Drew, I'm sorry," she apologised. "I was miles away.

"Don't worry. I think we've taken this as far as we can this morning. What do you think? Let's get Angela to type it up and get it off to Sir Max." He hesitated, a trace of concern in his voice. "Look Julia . . . I know this must be difficult for you. How about working half a day today and starting fresh tomorrow?"

"Don't Drew — I don't need any sympathy. I'll be OK. It's just that I haven't used my brain like this for so long." He was still looking serious. "Honestly it's OK," she said brightly.

Drew pushed back his chair and stood up flexing his shoulders. "What we both need is lunch. And if you're sure you want to stay . . . ?" he raised one dark brow questioningly.

"I'm sure. I want to stay."

"Thank goodness for that." He grinned. "There's all this to clear this afternoon," he gestured at his heaped desk "and I've a game of squash booked for this evening. Come on, I'm starving." He shrugged his jacket back on.

"By the way," Julia asked, "what time did you get in this morning?"

"Seven thirtyish. Didn't really notice the time. In the summer I come in early and then go jogging."

"Goodness, how energetic," Julia teased as they waited for the lift.

"Perhaps you'd like to come with me one morning," Drew suggested as the doors began to open.

Julia shook her head, laughing. "Oh no! Not my sort of thing at all — now if you'd said swimming you might have tempted me . . ."

She turned and stepped into the lift, straight into Jon's arms, the laughter still on her lips. He put his hands on her shoulders to steady her, his fingers warm through the fine fabric of her shirt.

"Welcome back Mrs Leyton," his eyes mocked down into hers. Welcome back into my arms, he meant — and they both knew it.

Julia was caught between the urge to stamp hard on his instep, and the desire to melt into his arms. She was saved from both by Drew's voice behind her demanding.

"Are you getting out at this floor, Farrell? If not, do you mind if we both get in?"

Jon ignored him. He dropped his hands from Julia's shoulders, but his eyes still held hers. She side-stepped quickly to join Drew on the other side of the lift. Damn Jon! Surely Drew couldn't have failed to notice the significance of that little by-play!

Rigid with embarrassment she stared at the far corner of the lift. Drew Scott was a man very much in control of himself, but she could feel him radiating irritation beside her.

Moments passed, then Jon commented, "I've no real objection to standing here all afternoon, but if you'd like to tell me which floor you want . . ."

"Ground," Julia said hurriedly before Drew could say anything. The last thing she wanted was to be caught in the middle of a row between these two on her first day back.

As they slowly descended towards the staff cafeteria Julia stole a covert look at Jon from under her lashes. In the first shock of finding herself in his arms she'd been unaware of anything but the sharp lime tang of his aftershave and the warmth of his eyes.

Now she realised she was seeing a Jon she'd never glimpsed before. Gone were the faded and creased khaki workclothes, the casual blue jeans and sweatshirt. He was wearing a deep navy summer-weight suit, a shirt so pale blue it was almost white, and a lemon silk tie.

He'd had a haircut. Julia tried to stop herself staring at the paler skin of his nape exposed by the hairdresser's scissors, the golden stubble which the sun hadn't bleached.

Jon looked the perfect executive, but

under the grooming Julia saw again the quality she'd recognised in Sir Max, the toughness, a controlled impatience with office life.

So why was he here, dressed like the other executives, the men he professed to despise? Had her comment yesterday about Max grooming Drew Scott as his successor hit home, made him determined to fight on Drew's ground?

The lift jolted to a halt. Julia, looking up suddenly, met his eyes and the memory she'd been trying to deny came flooding back, suffusing her face with hectic colour. In her mind they were back in the dim light of the cabin, his body hard and demanding against hers . . .

As the doors of the lift slid open Julia swung on her heel and almost ran towards the double doors of the cafeteria. Drew caught her up at the end of the queue for the self-service buffet. Julia kept her hot face averted from him as she filled her plate with food she didn't want. When they reached the till Drew held out money for both of them, then steered her towards a table on the now deserted balcony.

Julia pushed quiche round her plate in a desultory way, gathering her wits, searching for a neutral topic of conversation to cover her treacherous thoughts. How *could* she let her feelings for Jon get to her like that at work? Was it going to happen every time she saw him? Had Drew noticed anything?

"Julia," he began, cutting across her thoughts, "I realise I'm way out of line here, but it's obvious to me you've a real problem with Jon Farrell."

Julia glanced up quickly and saw the embarrassment on his face. "Drew, don't . . . "

"Let me say my piece," he cut in. "I realised there was antagonism between you, which I could understand — he's not an easy man . . . " his lips quirked in acknowledgement of his own past encounters with Jon Farrell, "but in the lift just now it was obvious there was more to it."

"Drew, please . . . I can't talk about it!"

"No Julia, let's get this out in the open. You of all people know we can't condone sexual harassment in the workplace."

Julia stared at him, fighting down a wild desire to laugh. How ironic! Here was Drew sure she was being sexually harassed, and all the time . . . She wondered what he'd say if he'd seen her on Saturday, returning Jon's kisses with an intensity which matched his own, ready to go wherever he led her.

"Drew, it's not what you think," she began.

"There's no need for you to feel guilty Julia," Drew interrupted firmly. "I happen to know Sir Max feels pretty strongly about this sort of thing."

"Stop it! He's not harassing me — emphatically not! At one point we were . . . close." The only way to shut Drew up was to give him some sort of convincing explanation, and if that meant bending the truth, she'd have to. "There's nothing between us now, but it's awkward when we meet . . . "

"Oh, I see. Well, that explains it; it's a pity he's around so much at the moment." Drew leaned back in his chair and sipped his coffee, more at ease now the air had been cleared.

"I don't want to make too big a thing of it," Julia explained, "it's just a pity I ran into him today when I'm so keyed up about coming back to work."

"Speaking of work," Drew glanced at his watch, "let's get back to it."

★ ★ ★

That night Julia slept like a log, exhausted by activity. The first week passed like lightning, her confidence growing with her work-load. People called to see her, her phone never stopped ringing. Her nervousness vanished, there was no time for it.

As for Jon — she made very sure she had no time to think about him either, but there was no avoiding him. She often glimpsed his rangy figure in the cafeteria, or leaving an office, but mercifully for her peace of mind there was no repeat of their close contact in the lift.

Julia was at her desk by eight o'clock on Monday. To her surprise she'd beaten Drew to it. When he came in half an hour later it was obvious he hadn't been jogging. He looked as immaculate as ever, but distinctly heavy-eyed.

"Morning Drew." Julia leaned back in her chair and smiled at him. "Take a lot of work home this weekend?"

"In a manner of speaking." He didn't elaborate.

"Sit down, I'll get you some coffee. You look as though you could do with some."

His hangover didn't impair his ability to work. He set a hard pace and by mid-afternoon they'd done a whole day's work. The rest of the week followed the same pattern; Julia sensed he was impatient to move on now he was confident she was back in control of things.

"Where do you go from here?" she asked on Wednesday while they were taking a break.

"Legal department, would you believe?" He grimaced. "I tried to look pleased when the Old Man told me yesterday, but I doubt if I fooled him."

"Well you can't expect to enjoy yourself all the time," Julia chided, laughing.

"Why not?" His voice seemed warmer suddenly, and there was an expression in his eyes she hadn't seen before.

Julia jumped to her feet. "It's no good, I'm going to go up and see Sir Max about this job description. Our first impression was right, he is asking for the impossible. See you in a minute."

Going up in the lift she wondered if she'd panicked, or even if she'd misinterpreted the warmth in Drew's eyes. This hopeless love for Jon threatened any friendship she might want to form with another man. Perhaps a civilised relationship with Drew might cure her . . . "

She'd left before checking with Sir Max's PA to see if he was free. Thankfully Sally was there.

"Is the boss free for five minutes?"

"I should think he'd welcome a break from what he's doing — you know how he hates checking the fine print on contracts." She pressed the intercom button. "Mrs Leyton to see you sir."

"Send her in."

From long experience of her boss Julia got straight to the point. "This job description. I'm afraid it's just not practical. We're asking too much for the money.

"Well, what do you suggest?"

Julia outlined the alternatives, ignoring the automatic scowl on her boss's face when he realised all of them would involve more money.

"I'll just leave these notes with you then sir . . . " She got up to go.

Sir Max waved the folder back at her. "Go on. You know what you're doing — do whatever you think's best. But just remember we're on a tight budget. Might be a good idea to send you to Accounts for six months and leave Scott in Personnel!"

Julia was still chuckling as she turned into the corridor. She was feeling on top of the world, in control of her job, in control of life again.

At the far end of the corridor a door opened and Jon walked out. He saw her and stood waiting until she drew level with him.

"Hello Julia." His face was inscrutable, his lips compressed into a firm line.

"Good afternoon Jon," she returned coolly.

"I'm glad I saw you. I was going to call round this evening." Still his face gave nothing away.

"Whatever for?" She saw his eyes narrow at her abruptness.

"To ask you to have dinner with me."

"No way! At least, not until you give me Danny's attaché case and a reasonable explanation as to why you've got it now, I don't know what your motives are Jon — but none of the explanations that occur to me are very creditable."

She'd finally demolished his sangfroid. He was angry now and it showed. "My motives! I don't think you give a damn about that briefcase. You used it as an excuse not to stay with me. What was it Julia — revenge for last time? There's a name for women who tease men — and I don't think you'd like me to use it."

Julia slapped him hard in blind reaction. Jon moved swiftly, his grip imprisoning both wrists as he jerked her hard against him.

"Don't play games with me Julia!" he blazed. "You deserve to be slapped right back."

Julia stared back appalled at the

reddening marks of her fingers on his cheek. She'd never seen any man so angry. The skin was taut across his cheek bones, a muscle jerked at the corner of his mouth, his eyes were dark as he fought for control.

She pulled back against his restraining grip, desperate to get away before they were seen by someone else. "Let's go of me," she hissed. "Remember where we are!"

Jon's response was immediate. He pulled her closer to his chest and kissed her ruthlessly, without the slightest pretence of desire. It was the one weapon in his armoury she couldn't counter. He released her as abruptly as he'd seized her, swept her from head to foot with a glance of icy dismissal and turned on his heel.

She was still raging inside when she got back to the office. Drew glanced round from the filing cabinet and stopped stock still when he saw her flushed cheeks and tousled hair.

"What on earth's the matter?" He

started forward. "You haven't had a row with the Old Man over that job description have you?"

"No," Julia ground out between clenched teeth. "Merely an encounter with Mr Farrell!" She touched her tender lips with the tip of her tongue, grimacing at the memory.

"He's really got your back up!" Drew seemed amused. "I never realised you had such a temper — what *did* he say to rile you?"

There was no way she could tell him Jon had accused her of being a calculating sexual tease! "He asked me to dinner," she blurted out, slamming the file down on her desk.

"You alarm me!" Drew grinned.

"Why?"

"Because I was going to ask you out but I'm not sure I dare now."

"Oh don't be ridiculous Drew!" Julia released her pent-up anger into laughter. "I'd love to have dinner with you."

"Saturday night OK?"

"Lovely. We'd better get back to work." She picked up the folder and passed it over to him. "Max grumbled a lot but he still OK'd the changes we wanted."

★ ★ ★

Drew handed the menu to the waiter and turned his attention back to Julia. "This was a good idea of yours, I love Indian food, but I haven't been here before."

Julia sipped her Martini, glancing round the small restaurant. "It's not been open long, and I thought somewhere informal would be more relaxing."

"We've certainly earned it," he agreed, raising his glass to toast her.

He was looking disturbingly attractive in a cream polo neck sweater and brown slacks. Julia had chosen a floaty silk shift she'd had made up from sari material Danny had brought back from a trip to India.

"The last two weeks must have

been tough for you," Drew observed. "You've got guts Julia — I really admire the way you've handled it."

"It was tough at first," she admitted. "Not just the job, but the whole discipline of working again. But I'm glad I did it." She smiled warmly at him, "And I'm glad it was you who helped me. Thanks Drew."

"It's been a pleasure. Now let's forget Faulkner's for a few hours! That dress is beautiful. It's an Indian fabric isn't it? Have you been out there?"

"No, but Danny was there for a short while."

"Yes, I remember. We were both involved with the same project, though we didn't actually meet. It's a fabulous country — you'd love it."

Drew was a natural raconteur. He made India alive for her, the exotic spices and scents of the meal completed the picture.

"I really enjoyed tonight," she said, slipping her arm through his as they walked towards his car. The evening air was balmy and the stars glittered in a clear sky. She felt warm, relaxed, slightly light-headed.

"It's not over yet," he remarked matter-of-factly as he unlocked the car door.

Julia's heart lurched. She hadn't thought beyond the end of the meal. What was he expecting? Did he want to be more than just friends — and if he did, how did she feel about it? At that moment she honestly didn't know.

"You're very quiet." Drew turned on to the road to the village.

"Just dreaming about India," she murmured. "Would you like to come in for coffee?"

As they walked up the path to her front door Julia searched in her handbag for her front-door key. She hoped Drew wouldn't read too much into her invitation.

"You could do with a light in this porch," he commented. "Let me help."

He leaned across her to turn the key in the lock, so close the soft wool of his sweater brushed her arm. She moved slightly towards him as the door clicked open, then they were suddenly dazzled by the harsh light of powerful car headlamps.

Drew turned sharply, one hand up to shield his eyes from the glare. "What the hell . . . ?"

With a sinking heart Julia recognised the throaty purr of the Jensen, then there was silence and darkness. She stumbled into the hall to switch on the light, the glare still imprinted on her retina.

Jon eased his long legs out of the car and strolled up the path to the front door.

"I'd have thought you were past the stage of kissing on the doorstep Julia." His teeth gleamed white in the subdued light, but there was no humour in his smile, or in his voice.

5

"I DON'T need lessons from you on how to behave Jon Farrell!" Julia flared. Damn the man for making her feel as if she and Drew were teenagers caught necking in the porch.

"Go away Jon." She was acutely aware of Drew moving to stand beside her, could feel the tension in his body. Unless she got rid of Jon quickly she was going to have a fight on her hands.

"I thought you wanted this urgently." He held up Danny's attaché case. "But, if you're too busy, I'll take it away again." He half turned.

"Of course I want it." Julia held out her hand. To her surprise Jon relinquished the case without comment. As soon as she felt the weight she knew why — it was empty.

Walking quickly into the brightness of the hall she rested it on the table, snapping open the locks to reveal the red silk lining and nothing else. There was not so much as a paperclip.

Julia swung round to find both men were in the hall. Drew's eyes flicked from her face to Jon's with wary appraisal, but very much on her side. Jon looked sardonic.

"It's empty! What have you done with the papers?"

"You asked me to return Danny's attache case. And that's exactly what you've got," he said dismissively. "Goodnight."

Julia stepped in front of him, her back to the door. "You're not going anywhere until you've told me what you've done with whatever was in that case. If it was Danny's I want it."

"I'm not going to discuss this in front of a third party." His eyes met hers with an unmistakable warning. Reluctantly Julia acknowledged the sense of what he was saying. If Danny had been bending the rules, however slightly, that wasn't something she wanted Drew to discover. His first loyalty would naturally be to the company.

She stood her ground, biting her lip in indecision until she saw the dawning suspicion in Drew Scott's eyes. Jon was right, it wasn't sensible to push him further now.

"While you're thinking about it Julia I'll let myself out of the back door." He turned and brushed past Scott as if he didn't exist. He paused on the threshold of the kitchen, a tall mocking figure all in black. "It's getting late and I want to go to bed — whatever your plans are."

Typical! she fumed. He couldn't resist the opportunity to slip in a dig at Drew. She avoided Drew's eyes: did he think that was why she'd invited him in? The back-door latch clicked and Jon was gone.

There was a pregnant pause, then Drew said, deadpan, "Makes himself at home, doesn't he?"

"He used to share the house with Danny, before we were married," Julia explained automatically. She couldn't think straight. She knew she ought to invite Drew to sit down, make coffee, try to patch up the evening, but still she stood here, back against the door.

"Julia . . . " Drew began uncertainly, then took her in his arms, brushing his lips lightly against hers.

"No . . . no Drew." Julia pulled back gently. She didn't want to hurt him but seeing Jon again, however angry he made her, forced her to realise she was still his.

"I'm sorry, that was inconsiderate . . . it's too soon for you. I'll go now." It was the first time she'd seen him at a loss.

"No. I'm sorry too. I don't know what I want myself Drew, and that isn't fair to you. Stay and have some coffee."

In the kitchen Julia filled the percolator and stood looking at her reflection staring back at her from the uncurtained window.

What game was Jon playing, turning up at this time of night with the case? Julia twisted the gold band on her finger. She was never going to feel easy about her short-lived marriage until she could be certain Danny had been happy. And only Jon, who'd been so close to him, held the key.

She could hear Drew moving about in the living-room. Poor man, she thought with a flicker of humour. Whatever he'd expected from this evening she doubted it would have included a midnight confrontation with Jon Farrell.

"Pour yourself a liqueur," she called. "The glasses are in the corner cupboard."

When she re-entered the living-room he was pouring whisky into a glass. "I've helped myself to your Scotch. I hope you don't mind."

Julia looked at him gratefully as she sank into an armchair. "You deserve a bottle of the stuff after what you've had to put up with tonight."

"Any time," he said easily, passing her a Benedictine. "Drink this and then I think you should get to bed." He took a sip from his own glass. "And I think I ought to stay here tonight. I'll sleep on the sofa," he added hastily as she glanced up in surprise. "I don't think you should be alone in the house after what's happened."

"I'm OK Drew, really. He isn't normally like that." And that was the truth, she wasn't simply saying it to quieten Drew's fears. What was driving Jon?

"If he's acting out of character, all the more reason for me to stay here. And if I went home and left you I'd only worry."

"I ought to refuse but I won't." It was easier to give in than to keep defending Jon's extraordinary behaviour. "I'm very grateful Drew."

Drew put his glass on the coffee table. "Come on. If you tell me where the blankets are I'll sort out a bed down here."

★ ★ ★

The buzz of the doorbell roused Julia from a deep, dreamless sleep. Muzzily she got up, groping for her dressing-gown. As she reached the head of the stairs she heard Drew's voice at the front door say wearily, "Oh no, not you again!" Julia moved down a couple of steps, looking through the banisters to see who Drew was talking to.

Drew was naked to the waist, a towel draped negligently over one shoulder. On the front doorstep she saw Jon, looking tired, unshaven and wearing the same black shirt and jeans as the night before.

The two men stared at each other in mutual antagonism until Drew threw a glance at an approaching milk-float and snapped, "You'd better come in. We're not doing Julia's reputation any good standing here."

"You might have thought of that last night," Jon remarked acidly, shouldering his way into the hall. "Is she up yet?"

"Yes I am." Julia came slowly down the stairs. Jon's thoughts were written all over his face; he believed she'd spent the night with Drew.

"Did I wake you?" He made it obvious he didn't really care.

"Oh no," she replied sarcastically. "I always sleep through two men snarling at one another on my doorstep!"

"There was something you wanted to discuss. So get rid of him and we'll discuss it," he commanded brusquely.

Drew met her eyes. "It's up to you Julia. I'll stay if you want — or," his voice hardened, "throw him out, with pleasure."

"Please! Both of you — stop it!" Julia gripped the banister. The combination of last night's emotion and the wine had left her with a thumping headache.

She took a deep breath and smiled at Drew. She hoped he'd understand that this was something between her and Jon alone. "I *have* got something to clear up with Jon, and the sooner the better." She reached out and touched his bare shoulder lightly. "Thank you for being here when I needed you . . . " She didn't care how that sounded to Jon.

Drew looked unconvinced. "Are you sure? I'll wait outside in the car if you like." Julia shook her head with a reassuring smile. "OK then, but I'll ring you later today." He picked up his sweater from the living-room and pulled it over his head. At the foot of the stairs he paused and to Julia's surprise took her gently into his arms, brushing his lips lightly over hers.

"What a touching little scene — very tender," Jon remarked laconically as the door closed behind Drew.

Julia swept past him into the kitchen, aching head held high. "You might find it difficult to understand, but I prefer Drew's tenderness to the way you last kissed me."

She plugged in the kettle, spooned

tea into the pot and dropped two Disprin into a glass of water.

Jon leaned against the door-frame watching her. "Got a hangover?"

"If I have that makes two of us by the look of you," Julia retorted. She'd never seen him look so ill, so unkempt. It was obvious he'd been drinking hard — and that was totally out of character.

"True. Make mine coffee — black."

She shot him a searching look but he'd already gone into the living-room. When she put the coffee down in front of him he was looking at the whisky bottle. "Hair of the dog?" he suggested.

Julia shuddered, the very thought of alcohol at that time of day making her queasy. "Oh no thank you! But have some if it'll make you feel better."

"Not unless you've got any brandy."

She found a bottle and handed it to him. "When did you have time to get a hangover?" And why? she thought.

"Most of last night." He tipped some

108

into his coffee and took a gulp.

"Why?" demanded Julia. "Because you were jealous of Drew?"

Jon leaned back in the chair, cradling the cup between his hands. She tried to see his face but he was looking down. "Why should I be jealous of who you sleep with? Jealousy implies an emotional involvement and as you keep telling me, ours — such as it is — is purely physical."

It was like a slap in the face. "I did not sleep with Drew Scott!"

Jon raised chilly blue eyes to hers. "You must think I'm a fool. What was he doing here last night — taking a shower?"

"I don't have to justify myself to you!" she flared back. "If you think I'm sleeping around that says more about your mind than it does about my morals!"

"I'm not suggesting you're sleeping around — just sleeping where it will do you the most good."

Julia couldn't believe her ears. "I

see," she found the words at last. "You've decided to believe the rumours about Drew Scott's prospects are accurate and you think so little of me you believe I'd sleep with him just because of that." Angry tears stung her eyes as she raised them to his sardonic face.

"I came here to talk about Danny — not your morals or lack of them."

Through her hurt and distress Julia recognised he was hurting and the knowledge dissolved some of her anger. Making these crazy accusations was giving Jon no pleasure. So what was driving him? Perplexed, Julia looked at his hard, set face and knew she wasn't going to get an apology out of Jon in this mood — but she might get nearer the truth about Danny. She'd failed on the boat, she couldn't give up now.

She crossed and knelt on the soft carpet in front of his chair, resting her hands on its arms, her expression grave and determined. "Just stop playing around Jon, you can't put me off by insulting me. I know you don't mean what you're saying. I need to know about Danny . . . why was he leaving Faulkner's? Why hadn't he told me? And what was in that attaché case?"

For a long moment Jon looked down at his hands, twisting the signet ring on his little finger. The fact he was fidgeting at all was an indication of the depths of his indecision.

"Yes I knew about the job. He was going to tell you when he came home on leave the next month. I think he wanted to tell you to your face — it would be such a big upheaval." His uncombed head came up, he looked her straight in the eye. "And you know Danny — he wanted to make a big thing of it, sweep you off for a mad celebration."

That's what she'd thought, but it still didn't ring true. Danny would never have been able to keep the secret, he'd have written. No, it was too pat. Jon was lying to her.

"Are you telling me he expected me

to go to Singapore with him?" she probed. That would explain why he'd been reluctant to tell her, she wouldn't have wanted to leave Faulkner's, and her travelling with him had never been a part of their bargain.

"I expect so," Jon said evasively.

"You haven't told me everything," she accused. "What was in the attaché case?" She gripped the arms of the chair and leaned towards him, willing him to be honest with her for once.

"There's not a lot I can tell you. Let's just say Danny played by his own rules." He let his head drop back on the cushions and closed his eyes, shutting out her intensity. "Did you love him very much?" The words came out harshly.

Julia swallowed hard. "Yes," she lied, her voice a whisper. What else could she say?

Jon gave a deep sigh and she realised incredulously that he was asleep, the coffee mug balanced precariously on his knee, his brown fingers still curled around the handle. There was no way of telling whether he had heard her reply.

Gently Julia prised the mug away from him. Now she could look at him without meeting that disconcerting blue stare she saw just how strained he looked. He'd lost weight, the skin was taut across his cheekbones, the lines of tension visible even under the stubble of his unshaven face.

Quietly she went back to her chair and curled up, sipping the now cold tea. She'd never seen him look so vulnerable, never loved him so much. She ached to take him in her arms, smooth away the worry lines around his eyes, kiss away the tiredness. And if she did he would open his eyes and she would see the rejection in them again. And that would be the end.

Emotion ebbed out of her, leaving her weary to the bone. Slowly she climbed the stairs and curled up on her bed. She was asleep almost before her head touched the pillow.

★ ★ ★

The chimes of an ice-cream van woke her at midday. Sunlight poured between the drawn curtains and lay in a hot bar across the bed. Julia rolled over stiffly and rubbed her eyes. Thank goodness, the dreadful, throbbing headache had gone.

She crossed to throw open the window, breathing deeply as the warm summer air blew into the room. Resting her forehead on the glass she gazed down on to the newly mown lawn. There was no car parked at the kerb, but in the state he'd been in this morning Jon would never have driven.

Julia padded barefoot to the top of the stairs and listened. Downstairs was all quiet; perhaps he'd left while she slept. She tiptoed down, peering through the banisters into the living-room. Jon hadn't moved.

She felt hot and sticky, her hair was in rats' tails and her lower lashes

114

were clogged with mascara. Upstairs she pulled a pile of fluffy fresh towels from the airing-cupboard, and turned on the shower.

The hot water sluiced through her hair, over her shoulders and down her back. Julia shampooed her hair into a foam of lemon scented bubbles, let them trickle down her spine while she soaped herself rigorously with a bath mitt. She held up her face to the stinging jets and let the soap rinse away over her toes.

After a vigorous towelling Julia dusted on a cloud of *Ivoire* talc and combed her wet hair off her face, twisting it up on top of her head with a single pin. Draping the biggest bath sheet round her she drifted out into her bedroom, humming softly under her breath. She was feeling better, but she didn't know why. Nothing had changed. But somehow just having him here in the house was enough to lighten her heart.

The sound of footsteps on the landing

sent her to the door, one hand on the knob to push it closed, then she saw Jon standing at the top of the stairs, his arms full of the bedclothes Drew Scott had taken down the night before.

Their eyes met over the heap of blankets, his rueful and wary, hers uneasy in the face of his obvious penitence. Jon judgemental and accusing she could cope with, but not Jon filled with self-reproach.

"I've a fairly hazy recollection of what I said this morning, but what I can remember is pretty unforgivable. Just tell me where to put these and I'll go." His voice was husky.

"In the spare bedroom," she responded automatically. Jon brushed past her and dumped his burden in the end room. She watched as he straightened up, stretching the taut muscles of his back then letting his broad shoulders drop in resigned gesture.

Julia was so aware of his body language it signified more to her than his actual words. But what did he feel for her? They weren't friends, they weren't lovers, but they weren't enemies either, all she knew was she couldn't let him go like this.

As he passed her to go down the stairs she reached out and touched his arm. "Jon . . . we can't leave it like this." He stopped, hands jammed deep in the pockets of his jeans. Through her fingertips his tension vibrated like signals down a wire.

"You're right." He met her gaze squarely. "I shouldn't have said what I did about Scott spending the night here."

"You say that now you've found the evidence that he didn't share my bed," she responded bitterly.

"I don't care whether he did or not. That's none of my business. You don't need me, Scott, anyone else other than on your own terms." Suddenly his voice was vehement. "You've put yourself back together alone. I had no right to undermine that process. I should have stayed out of your life — I will from now on."

Julia reacted without thinking, throwing her arms round his chest, hugging him fiercely. "Oh Jon, we're such idiots," she muttered. "Why can't we just be friends?" It felt so good to be holding him she'd settle for whatever he was offering.

Jon held her away from him, his weary face transformed by laughter. "You stand there in a damp bath towel looking utterly edible and ask me to be . . . just good friends?"

"Well *you* look like a walking health hazard!" she laughed back, pushing him towards the bedroom mirror. "Look at yourself!"

"I wouldn't have believed I could look as bad as I feel — but I do." He ran his hand through his thick, tousled hair. "I need a shower."

"Help yourself." Julia gestured towards her bathroom. "I'll get you some fresh towels."

Steam was already clouding the room when she returned moments later. Jon's tanned body was a dark silhouette against the frosted glass of the shower door, both hands raised lathering his hair.

He wouldn't want to come out smelling of *Ivoire*. Julia unwrapped a bar of lemon scented soap and tapped on the door. "Take this, the soap in there's perfumed."

Jon slid back the door to its full extent, snaked out one wet, brown arm and before she could blink she was under the shower with him, towel and all.

Through the steam his grin was wide and teasing. Water coursed down his face, streaking his darkened hair against his head, sheeting off his muscular shoulders and taut hips.

Julia gasped, the breath knocked out of her by the onslaught of the water, the swiftness of his movement, the proximity of his naked body to hers.

"What . . . ?"

He reached out and released the wet folds of towelling from her body, laughing down into her startled face. "What did you say about soaping my back?"

"Nothing," she said helplessly, then collapsed into giggles.

He turned his back. "What are you waiting for? Get scrubbing!"

His ridiculous mood was infectious and laughter the cure for the intensity and pain of the last twelve hours.

"You asked for it," she warned, seizing the friction mitt and attacking his shoulders vigorously. She kneaded and rubbed mercilessly, forcing him to spreadeagle against the tiled wall, ignoring his laughing protest until his back gleamed pink.

She didn't falter until she reached his waist, the sleek symmetry where his long body met the narrow strength of his hips. The childlike game had suddenly become very adult.

Jon was very still. All she could hear was the water pounding on the shower floor, echoing the pounding of her heart in her breast. Her hands rested either side of his waist, the soap and mitt dropping down disregarded.

Jon covered her hands with his, drawing them round to rest against the flat muscles of his stomach. His pulse leapt under her mouth as she trailed blind kisses down the line of his shoulder. She was drowning . . . drowning . . . but they were going down together.

★ ★ ★

The stinging water brought Julia slowly back to the surface. It seemed hours later, she had no way of telling how much time had passed. She opened her eyes and saw Jon searching her face as if seeing her for the first time.

Julia could find no words to answer that look. She smiled tremulously at him, on the brink of tears. Jon turned off the shower. The silence was almost deafening. The next thing she knew she was being swathed in towels, carried into the bedroom, laid gently on the bed.

Her eyelids drooped. At the edge of consciousness she could hear Jon moving around, then the bed dipped under his weight as he stretched out his long body next to hers. With a sigh he turned over, moulding his body against hers, one heavy arm possessively keeping her close. Her body warm, formless, she drifted off to sleep.

Julia woke first. Jon had rolled over in his sleep and lay face down, arms sprawled on the pillow, head averted. His rib cage rose and fell slowly as he slept. Careful not to wake him Julia sat up, curled against the headboard and watched him. The first time she'd slept with him she'd woken relaxed and vulnerable to find the bed beside her cold and empty. Last time they'd parted in silence, misery on her part, coldness on Jon's.

This time, at least until he woke, he was all hers and she was going to savour the luxury, save up the memory. For a few moments she could pretend that he loved her too.

The late afternoon light slanted across the room throwing a thick gold stripe across the smooth, burnished skin of Jon's back. Julia couldn't resist bending to trace a parallel path with her lips, tasting the salt sheen of sweat on his sun-warmed body.

Jon shifted in his sleep, a sensual shiver rippling the muscles under her mouth. She slid down against his flank, sensing his gradual return to consciousness. He murmured her name, "Julia?" and turned, gathering her in his arms.

She melted into his embrace, her lips blindly seeking his. Jon kissed first one corner of her mouth, then the other, tenderly teasing her before he claimed the full soft curve completely. His chest rose and fell against hers in a deep contented sigh as one hand stroked through her hair gathering the heavy fullness in his fingers.

"Julia darling . . . " he whispered against her throat.

"Jon . . . " she whispered in response. "Oh Jon . . . "

The phone rang shattering the precious moment like glass. Jon cursed under his breath and lunged to knock off the receiver but Julia grabbed it just in time, dropping an apologetic kiss on his shoulder as she did so.

"Julia Leyton speaking. Oh, Drew . . . no, no, I'm fine, just a little sleepy . . . " It didn't sound a very convincing excuse, even to her.

Jon got off the bed and strode into the bathroom pulling a face at her that made her giggle.

"Are you OK?" Drew sounded surprised.

"Yes perfectly," Julia replied happily. There was the buzz of an electric razor from the bathroom, its note rising as Jon strolled back into the room, his body partially covered by a towel round his waist. "Go away," she mouthed at him.

124

There was a puzzled silence from Drew, then he said rather stiffly, "Well, if you're sure . . . I'll see you on Monday then."

"Goodbye." Julia dropped the receiver. "Jon! How could you — what Drew must have thought!"

He grinned unrepentantly. "Let him think. There are some things I don't mind sharing with Drew Scott . . . " he indicated the razor, "and some I do!"

"Jon!" she protested, "I've already told you I didn't sleep with him. There's nothing between us, he's just a friend."

"And I thought I'd made it clear I didn't care either way — it's just I could do without him on the phone when I'm in bed with you."

Julia went very still, his words hitting her like a douche of cold water. So, what she'd mistaken for tenderness had merely been the afterglow of their love-making. He didn't even care enough to be jealous. Jon was in the bathroom pulling on his clothes, unable to see the stricken look on her face. She felt winded, as if someone had hit her hard in the stomach.

Julia scrambled off the bed and dressed quickly, pulling on jeans and a T-shirt. Fully dressed too, Jon came and put his arms round her. Julia twisted free and paused in the doorway. "Would you like some tea before you go?"

Jon's face hardened at the dismissive note in her voice. He tugged a lock of still-damp hair in mock deference. "Thank you your ladyship. Do I get a tip for services rendered too?" There was no mistaking the anger in his voice, or on his face.

"Don't be so unreasonable Jon," she said coldly. "You don't expect me to pretend there's anything more to what's happening than a little physical pleasure do you?" It came out sounding hard, harsher than she'd intended. "I've got things to do today, and no doubt you have too. That was just 'unfinished business' I think you called it the other day. Now there's no reason for us to meet again."

The look on his face was enigmatic. "I wouldn't be too sure about that Julia." Then he was gone.

6

JULIA stared tiredly at the file in front of her, the words and figures blurring. It was hopeless. She looked at her watch in despair — half past nine and she'd done nothing despite being in the office for two hours. Her brain felt bruised from a night of restlessness broken by vivid dreams of Jon's face as he'd left her.

She'd woken to find herself reaching out for him in the wide empty bed, despising herself for her subconscious fantasies. Eventually she'd abandoned the idea of sleep and had gone downstairs to roam round the garden in the early morning light until she could leave for the office.

But being awake was as bad as dreaming. Jon's face haunted her, unfathomable, unreadable. If only she could understand what their relationship

128

really meant to him.

And she missed Drew, missed his companionship and his support, his good humour. She'd looked forward to her first week by herself, to really being back in charge, but the pleasure had turned to ashes. Julia pushed back her chair and got up to look out of the window. Miles of rolling Berkshire fields provided neither distraction nor solace. If only she knew when Jon was going overseas again . . . If she was no longer in danger of bumping into him at any moment it would be easier to put him out of her mind. Perhaps there was something in his file.

She opened the filing cabinet, flicking through until she came to his personal record. Julia skimmed quickly past the early pages, head bent in concentration as she walked slowly back to her desk. She'd forgotten the extra desk set at right-angles to her own until she cracked her hip painfully on its sharp edge.

Her irritation crystallised — at last

she had something to be angry at. She flicked the switch on the intercom, "Angela! Come in here please!"

The secretary wasn't used to such a brusque tone and it showed on her face.

"I thought I asked you on Friday to get Maintenance to move that thing!" Julia pointed at the offending piece of furniture.

"Yes you did, but then Mr Farrell told me to leave it," Angel responded, looking pained.

"Since when have you taken orders from Jon Farrell?" Julia demanded.

"Since nine o'clock this morning," Jon's voice said smoothly from the doorway. He was once more an immaculate businessman, worlds apart from either the ashen-faced contrite Jon or the sensitive, passionate lover. The only thing that remained from yesterday was the anger, cold and glittering.

"We'll see about that!" Julia's full summer skirt swirled as she stalked towards the door. "I'm not standing for interference in my department!"

Jon remained in the doorway, unmoved by her vehemence. Over his shoulder he said, "Thanks Angela. There are some files in Sally Webster's office I need; she knows which ones. Get them for me will you. I'll buzz if I need you."

Angela shut the door hastily. "Who do you think you are!" Julia demanded, her hazel eyes sparking fire. "How dare you order my secretary out of the room?"

"Do you really want her in here while we have a stand-up fight? Fine, let's call her back."

"I've no intention of having a fight, I'm just waiting for you to get out of my way so I can go and ask Sir Max what authority you have for throwing your weight around in my department."

"I'm here on Sir Max's authority. And I'm not throwing my weight around — merely attempting to do my job." His voice was flat and hard.

Julia recognised the anger again, but it wasn't centred on her. This anger was clinical, intellectual, the anger of a man thwarted in his work. He'd just come from Sir Max therefore, Julia reasoned, the Old Man was the target for his anger.

"What do you mean? Office space in this building isn't so short engineers have to move in with Personnel!" she retorted.

"Sharing an office is the most efficient way of working together on a joint project. And that's precisely what you and I will be doing for the next month." The thought obviously gave Jon no pleasure. He dropped his long frame into the chair at the spare desk and crossed his arms.

"What project?" Julia stared at him bewildered, then his parting shot yesterday came back to her and she made the connection. "You knew! You knew yesterday and you didn't tell me!" She planted both hands on his blotter and leaned across the desk, challenging him to deny it.

"Yes I knew. I knew on Friday. But I thought we'd be liaising for four days, not working together for four weeks."

"But aren't you due to go back to the site!" To think this morning she'd been worried she might see him occasionally . . . now she'd got to work with him!

"I was expecting to go back next week." Jon's mouth was a hard line of disgust. "Now it appears I'm needed here and someone else can finish what I've sweated blood over for months." He was making no attempt to hide his bitterness.

"No, I won't do it," Julia stated emphatically. "I'm going up to tell the boss that now."

Her hand was already twisting the door knob when he said, "If I were you I'd consider what excuse you're going to give him before you get in there."

Julia turned, her eyes narrowed with suspicion. "What have you told him?"

"Me? Nothing. I'm just intrigued to know how you're going to handle Sir Max. I warn you, he's not in a good mood now . . . "

"Just because you've had a row with him doesn't mean he won't listen to me!" she fired back.

"Listen to you telling him what? That we were lovers?" Jon stood and moved towards her as he spoke. "That you'd like him to ship me back out to the desert so you won't be tempted?" His voice was soft and insinuating. Julia backed up against the door, holding up her hands to fend off his words, the nearness of his body.

"Stop it," she whispered. "Stop it. Let me go!" But it was too late, he was kissing her with passionate intensity. He captured her face between his palms as he deepened the kiss and Julia's anger dissolved.

One rational thought remained: someone might come in. She reached blindly for the small catch on the door knob and clicked it home. At the sharp sound Jon freed her mouth, then stepped back leaving her leaning against the door. "What are you doing?"

"Locking the door, of course. What if someone comes in?"

"So what if they had? That was as far as I intended going. That was unfinished business, something we had to get out of the way. Now either go upstairs and tell Sir Max why you won't work with me, or start acting like a professional. We've got a lot of work to do."

Scarlet with humiliation Julia fled to the small cloakroom next to her office, slammed the door shut behind her and shot the bolt home. Jon had used that kiss to prove a point. And because she loved him it had worked as it always did when he took her in his arms. But there couldn't be a clearer demonstration that what was between them for him was only desire.

She opened her locker and took out her make-up bag and a small towel, running cold water into the handbasin, splashing her burning complexion until the colour ebbed.

"Well, what are you going to do now?" she asked her reflection. Jon was right: there was no way she could go to Sir Max and insist he move him from her office. So she'd have to work with him what ever it was. Could this be the big project the boss had hinted at? There was no getting out of it, therefore she'd have to see it through with every ounce of professionalism and dignity she possessed. But, she vowed, never again would she drop her guard with him.

Julia smoothed foundation on her face, steadied her lips with a bold, bronze lipstick and brushed out her hair until it crackled. She paused for a moment, breathing deeply like an actress then re-entered her office. Angela, stacking files in Jon's in-tray, gave her a searching look which she returned with a small smile.

Jon ignored her presence until the secretary had left the room, then looked up. "Well? Are we working together or not?"

"Suppose you tell me what it's about?" Damn the man! He knew she hadn't been up to Sir Max. Couldn't he show the vaguest sign of emotion?

"You remember that Brazilian transportation project there were rumours about last year?"

"But the Board decided not to tender, didn't it?" Julia twisted in her chair to face him. If he could act as though nothing had happened, then so must she. "The word was it was too big for us, we didn't have the resources to cope with it."

"We still don't — alone, but the boss has been wheeling and dealing behind the scenes, and he's set up a consortium."

"How did the Board take him going behind their backs?" Julia asked.

"He told me they were furious at first — until he showed them the figures. Then they were all for it," he added.

"The crafty old fox! He really does

enjoy taking risks, doesn't he?"

Jon shrugged. "When you've been in the field a desk job is pretty tame. He misses the excitement. Manipulating a few elderly directors is small beer by comparison."

Julia glanced at him from under her lashes. He was right about Sir Max, but he was talking about himself. Would any woman ever tie him down?

"What are you thinking about?" Jon asked, curious.

"Just considering where we fit in," she said quickly.

"You've made your mind up then?"

"It sounds interesting enough to be worth putting up with you," she responded sweetly.

He ignored her sarcasm. "This is going to mean an enormous recruitment drive, we'll need engineers and technical staff in specialities we've never touched before. And we need to liaise with the other members of the consortium on everything from advertising to welfare." He slapped his palm on the pile of folders in front of him. "You're handling the personnel side of course."

"And you?" Julia queried. Despite everything she couldn't suppress her rising excitement at the thought of getting her teeth into such an important project as this.

"I'll be providing the technical back-up all the way through the recruitment phase — job profiles, interviewing, liaison with the other firms involved. *Then* I can get back in the field." He leaned back in his chair and studied her face for her reaction.

"And you'll be chief engineer," she stated. Jon nodded. "Then why . . . " Julia queried, thinking aloud, "why were you so furious when you came down from seeing the boss?"

She was aware of Jon weighing his answer carefully. Even before he spoke she knew he wouldn't tell her everything. "He was giving me a hard time over the last job," he said eventually.

The contract he was on with Danny, the job he was expecting to return to and finish. "What's wrong?" Julia probed uneasily.

"Just that he thought I was dragging it out at the end; that I should have handed over to someone more junior to finish up at least a couple of months ago." He got up and moved restlessly to look out of the window, his fists clenched in his pockets.

"And should you have?" Had he spun out the job deliberately to avoid coming home? There was more to this than he was telling her.

Jon turned back from studying the view and said lightly, "I don't think so. He did. It's academic now anyway. Let's have coffee and start work on this lot," he indicated the files.

He began to sort through them, tossing most of them to one side. "There's a copy of the briefing file with all the background information amongst this lot somewhere," he muttered.

Julia waited, her eyes resting on his

140

blond head, so groomed, so different from the wayward mane she associated with him. His fingers were sure and confident as he flicked through the papers, the strong tendons standing out against the tan an English summer was doing nothing to lessen.

I may love him but I'll never understand him, she thought despairingly. He was a mass of contradictions: passionate and controlled, kind and cruel, hard yet with a disarming vulnerability he hid almost too well. But then Jon hid all his emotions: a lesson she was learning the hard way.

Jon wasn't the marrying kind, but Danny had been. He was in the UK on a six-month secondment when Jon had walked out on her. At first she'd thought he was just being kind. One night over dinner at their favourite restaurant he'd asked her how she felt about marriage.

"In theory?" she'd asked, half joking, half bitter. "Fine — if two people love and trust each other."

"No, not in theory, in practice."
Danny's dark eyes were serious, intent,
"I want you to be my wife. Marry me
Julia."

He took her hand across the table,
his fingers stroking her palm. "I know
you've been badly hurt. I know you'll
never love me the way you love him."

She'd felt the colour rising in her
cheeks. "Wouldn't it matter to you that
Jon and I have been lovers?"

"There are skeletons in my cupboard
too. But I'm talking about us, now.
I want a wife who's a companion, a
friend, not just a lover. I want children
— and so do you Julia. And you'll
never have them if you spend your
whole life waiting for a man you'll
never possess.

At first she'd laughed, refused to take
him seriously, but he'd persisted every
time they met, demolishing all her
resistance with the argument it would
be best for both of them.

"But you'll be away so much," she'd
protested one afternoon.

"I'll be home on leave and it won't be for ever. I'll have my work and you'll have yours — and the children. It will give me something to look forward to when I come home." He was so sincere, so warm and so persistent.

"You seem able to put your life into separate compartments," Julia had observed.

Danny shrugged. "Basic survival technique, otherwise you'd spend all your time wishing you were somewhere else. Anyway, for the moment I've got no choice — but if I had you to come home to . . . " He kissed her fingertips, his voice suddenly husky. "Say yes Julia, I need you . . . "

"When you're quite ready . . . " Jon's sardonic tone snapped her back to the present. Julia felt the hot colour staining her cheeks, took a rapid gulp of cold coffee and dragged her mind back to the job in hand. The only way she was going to survive the next month was to keep her mind on the job.

She needn't have worried. That first week there was no time to think of Jon as anything but a colleague, demanding her opinion, teaching her things about the engineering industry.

Another secretary was seconded from the typing-pool to help Angela deal with the mass of paperwork. All week they worked late. At the end of each day Jon went his way and Julia went hers although the secretaries often went for a drink or a meal together.

The second week was less hectic but no less pressured. Julia acknowledged Jon's absolute professionalism; between them they'd established routines, a pattern of work meshing his skills with hers. She would never have believed it possible they could work together like this.

Jon paid her the compliment of not commenting on her competence. Each day he pushed her harder, expected more and each day he got it, and in return she drew on his skills and strengths. Julia never once saw him irritated or put out.

"I believe you're unflappable!" she joked after one disastrous morning when everything seemed to go wrong from the phones to the coffee machine, and finally the air-conditioning.

Jon grinned. "To quote the Duke of Wellington — 'Tie a knot and carry on!' This is mild compared to what can happen on site, believe me."

They were reaching the point where they needed to set up a meeting with their partners in the project. Julia tapped the list with her pen. "We're happy with this now?"

"It's fine with me," he concurred, "but I bow to your superior knowledge in these matters." He meant it, too. She'd seen no sign of the old sardonic Jon since they'd begun working together. He might be the more senior member of the firm but he always deferred to her area of expertise.

"I'll take it up to the boss then." Julia stood up, giving a little moue of distaste at her shirt sticking damply to the small of her back. "Give Maintenance a ring will you and chase them up about this air-conditioning. They might take some notice of you."

Jon produced a screwdriver and marched purposefully to the window. "I'm going to try a little old-fashioned ventilation first," he announced. "These windows must open somehow."

Pausing to splash some cologne on her wrists, Julia watched him sizing up the problem, fists on hips, eyes narrowed in concentration as he figured out how to open the hermetically sealed panes. Since the breakdown of the air-conditioning in their block the day before he'd abandoned his suit for short-sleeved shirts and tailored slacks. This was how he must be on site, grappling with a practical problem totally absorbed.

I like him so much when he's like this, she thought wistfully; this was how he'd been when they'd first met but there was no going back now.

"Ah ha!" John exclaimed trium-
phantly, attacking the seal round the
frame in a way that would make
Maintenance blench. Julia smiled, and
left.

★ ★ ★

"That's fine, give the list of people
you want to meet to Sally. I'll get
her to set up a series of meetings next
week, she's already in touch with the
chief engineers of the other consortium
members. They'll be here next week
too." Sir Max leaned back in his deep
leather chair and steepled his fingers.

Julia shifted uneasily under his
penetrating gaze. It wasn't like the
boss to sit in contemplation when
there was work to be done. What was
he working up to?

"How are you getting on with
Farrell?" he asked abruptly.

"Fine. We work together perfectly
well." That at least was true, but she
was flustered by the question; it was

utterly out of character for Sir Max to concern himself with relationships between colleagues. It was obvious he knew something had occurred between her and Jon, but how much?

"Good," he said eventually. "Well, what are you hanging round here for?"

"Nothing Sir Max, thank you." She left quickly before he said anything more.

"What the devil was the old so-and-so getting at?" she wondered aloud. Surely Jon couldn't have told him anything? No, impossible. A horrible thought occurred to her — had he picked up office gossip? The possibility that anyone had guessed she and Jon had been lovers made her go hot all over.

Taking a mound of work home over the weekend helped keep Julia's mind off the worry that everyone in the office knew about her private life. What was even more galling was the fact that relations between the two of them had been perfectly correct for the last fortnight — and showed every sign of staying that way.

Monday morning dawned, still and stifling. Julia got up at six, already uncomfortably hot. She showered and scoured her wardrobe for something cool enough to survive the day in. For the last fortnight she'd dressed carefully, avoiding the slightest hint of allure in what she wore. But today she'd have to dress for the heat even if that meant something skimpier than she usually wore for work.

She checked her appearance in the full-length mirror before she left at seven. The sundress was full-skirted, with a fitted top and narrow rouleaux straps. The cool pistachio colour emphasised the green in her eyes, highlighted her new golden tan.

Jon was already at his desk, his tie discarded. "You too!" He gestured at his watch. "This is going to be a long hot day if every thing's going to be ready for the Wednesday meeting."

"It will be," Julia replied crisply.

"It has to be! Pass me that salaries spreadsheet will you?"

There was a tap on the office door. From where she was standing by the filing cabinets Julia saw Jon glance up, saw the unwelcoming set of his face and guessed who it was even before Drew Scott's voice asked, "Is Julia around?"

"Yes." Jon obviously didn't give a damn how curt he sounded.

Julia came round the corner, her full skirt swirling against her legs. Jon dropped his eyes to the papers littering his desk, pointedly ignoring the interchange between the two of them.

"Hello Drew." Her greeting was friendly, but not overly so. She hadn't spoken to him since that Sunday afternoon when Jon had made love to her in the shower.

"I called by to see if you'd join me for lunch," he invited.

"I'm sorry Drew, but I can't. Look at my desk! We're snowed under. Another day perhaps." Just then Angela came in with a tray of sandwiches and coffee, underlining the point.

"See what you mean!" Drew said ruefully. "Sometime next week perhaps. Bye."

Despite her cool tone Julia was rattled. Every time she thought of Drew she remembered the last time she'd spoken to him, when he'd phoned her after she and Jon had made love in the shower. How had she sounded? He must have recognised the sound of the electric razor. What had he thought? It was too much to hope he'd imagined her shaving her legs!

Julia smiled, then sobered immediately Jon glanced at her. It would have been fun to share the joke, but that last ruthless kiss had widened the gulf between them.

"Have a sandwich," she passed him the plate, "and don't pinch all the egg and cress this time!" Her tone was light, but it didn't dissipate the slight atmosphere that had developed with Drew's appearance.

The day got progressively hotter, stickier, more humid. At seven it became obvious they still had another couple of hours work in front of them. Julia had sent Angela home.

"We're going to need to eat," Jon announced. "And I could do with a drink. I'm going up to the top floor, see what I can scrounge from the fridge."

Julia eased her aching body out of the chair and went and washed her hands and face. Her hair had started to kink in the humidity, and where it rested on her shoulders the skin prickled with perspiration. When she got back Jon was pouring a spritzer, mixing the cold mineral water with white wine. "Heaven!" Julia sighed, taking a deep drink, then rolling the cool glass against the damp skin of her forehead.

"Are you up to working on?" Jon looked at her with concern.

"Yes, I'll be OK when I've got some food inside me. What did you find?"

"*Voilà!* Two seafood salads from the executive fridge."

"That looks delicious." Julia took a forkful. "I adore *calamari*."

The impromptu meal washed down with half a bottle of Hock, relaxed them both. They worked on solidly, poring over the costings for the increased staffing.

"Well if that doesn't satisfy the Old Man nothing will," Julia declared, perching on the edge of Jon's desk as she clicked off her calculator.

"Quite frankly I don't give a damn!" Jon leaned back in his chair, his eyes closed. Julia saw the fatigue in his face, the lines around his mouth, the pale skin under his eyes. Spontaneously she reached a hand to brush back the lock of hair falling across his forehead. Her fingertips touched the damp skin in a gesture that became a caress before she could prevent it.

Without opening his eyes Jon's fingers curled round her wrist, drawing her palm down to meet his lips, kissing the sensitive centre, tracing the base of her thumb with the tip of his tongue.

Julia's breathing slowed, suspended by the incredible intimacy of the action. Gradually his eyelids opened. His eyes holding hers burned with a blue intensity she'd never seen before. His mouth was warm and sensual against her palm, his lips murmuring against her skin.

How long they sat there joined by the wordless communion of their eyes Julia had no idea. All she was aware of was a surging wave of joy sweeping through her, the dawning realisation that in Jon's eyes there was an answering emotion to the one now filling her.

His lips moved, forming her name. "Julia . . ."

The phone shrilled, shattering the brittle moment. Julia jumped to her feet, her heart in her mouth with the shock.

"Hell and damnation!" Jon snatched up the receiver. "Farrell," he snarled.

She stood holding the edge of her

desk for support, hardly able to believe what had just passed between them. Her mind was a whirl with the implications of what she'd seen in Jon's face.

It took a moment before his words penetrated her daze. "I can't talk now," he was saying, low-voiced into the phone. The voice at the other end protested, unmistakable feminine. "All right . . . " he conceded, "as soon as I can make it, but not now."

A cold hand gripped Julia's heart as she took in the expression on Jon's shuttered face, heard the guarded way he was responding to the woman on the other end of the line.

"Give me the number. I'll ring you later." He scribbled some figures on the desk pad and hung up. Avoiding Julia's eyes he slipped the number in his jacket pocket and stood up.

She had too much pride to let him see how terribly she was hurting. She pushed files into her case at random, desperate to get away. Whoever the woman was, she was important enough to obliterate what had just passed between them. And that meant only one thing, Julia decided bitterly. They were lovers, and that phone call had saved her from making a terrible fool of herself, embarrassing them both by blurting out her love for him.

"I don't know what time I'll be in tomorrow," he stated baldly as they locked the office door behind them.

Of course not, thought Julia starkly, he'll be with that woman, in her arms, tasting her kisses. Julia didn't need to use her imagination to picture the scene only her memory.

7

JULIA drove home with fierce concentration, the mechanical actions of steering, changing gear, braking, filling up the void in her mind, keeping at bay the thought of Jon in that other woman's arms.

She dropped her keys on the hall table, walked through to the living-room and curled up in the window-seat hugging her knees to her chest in a protective curve.

Outside, lightning flashed across a blackening sky. In the distance she could hear the rumble of thunder. She felt desolate, beyond tears. Just when she was sure she'd seen love in his eyes, she'd discovered all over again that for Jon their relationship was just a game.

The storm broke overhead with a crash that shook the windows and suddenly she found she could cry. But even when the tears had stopped the pain remained. Being older, more experienced, hadn't made her any wiser in her dealings with Jon. He had someone else, someone he must have been planning to meet when he'd carried her to the bed with so much tenderness.

★ ★ ★

"But I can't leave the office today. Jon's not in yet and there's too much to do!"

Sir Max's bushy eyebrows rose at her vehemence. "I'm perfectly well aware of that, and he's not at home either." He didn't bother to hide his annoyance. "He's the obvious person to pick up Cline's senior engineer."

Julia knew she was looking mulish. "But I hate driving in London. Why can't someone else pick up this Dr Fredericks?"

"Because I'm sending you!" Her

boss's tone brooked no argument. "The poor chap's been sent over at a moment's notice anyway. I got some garbled message about Paul Cline — he's broken his leg or something. Apparently Fredericks is the deputy, it's only a matter of courtesy to send someone senior to collect him — I shouldn't need to tell you that."

The reprimand was deserved, but the thought of having to battle through the London traffic made her feel even worse than she did already. She'd sat at the window until the sky was streaked scarlet by the dawn, and only then had fallen into bed for a couple of hours' restless sleep.

The drive in was every bit as bad as she expected. Julia always hated driving in central London, hated the ill-tempered, aggressive attitude of her fellow road users. By the time she drew up outside the Royal Park Hotel she'd already been carved up by three taxis and a bus in her journey round Hyde Park Corner.

It was a relief to hand over the BMW to the uniformed doorman and see it parked for her. In no mood to window shop she marched past the glossy lobby boutiques and headed straight for the reception desk. She just hoped Dr Fredericks was ready to go, she didn't want to hang around.

"Madam?" the desk clerk enquired.

"I'm from Faulkner Engineering, I'm here to collect Dr Fredericks."

"Ah yes, she's expecting you. Suite 606 on the third floor."

Julia got into the lift, her spirits rising. A woman engineer was still unusual enough: one this senior would be interesting to meet. It might not be such a bad journey back after all, and this morning especially she felt she'd had enough of the entire male sex.

She walked down the carpeted corridor and knocked firmly on 606. A strong, mid-Atlantic voice called, "Come in." Julia pushed open the door and stepped into a small living-room. A tanned woman with cropped blonde

160

hair was sitting on the sofa pouring coffee.

"I'm from Faulkner's." Julia held out her hand.

The other woman stood up and took it in a cool, firm handshake. She was about thirty-five, taller than Julia, slim but with the strong shoulders of an athlete. Julia noticed that underneath the light make-up she looked tired, heavy-eyed; it was the only thing that marred the impression of tough vitality.

"Gloria Fredericks. Good to meet you, but I'm afraid you've had a wasted journey — I should have rung your office earlier. Please, sit down, have a cup of coffee, Ms . . . ?"

"Oh, sorry," Julia smiled and sat down, "I'm Julia L . . . "

The words died on her lips as Jon emerged from the bedroom, buttoning his shirt, his hair damp from the shower. "Was that room service with the razor?"

He saw Julia, saw the stunned expression on her face, swore softly then demanded, "What the hell are you doing here?"

There was no need to ask him the same question, Julia thought through the ache of misery; she knew damned well what he'd been doing there.

Jon moved to Gloria's side and said with strange emphasis, "This is Julia Leyton, Danny's widow." A silence followed Jon's flat introduction. Gloria's face went blank as she looked at Jon, then the tension was broken by a knock at the door and the entrance of a waiter carrying a tray with fresh coffee and an electric razor.

"Put it down anywhere." Jon gestured towards the low table. "Thanks." He handed the man a tip, waiting until the door shut behind him before saying, "Make mine black."

Julia bit her lip, determined not to let him see the pain tearing her apart. She wanted to turn tail and run, only her pride and social convention kept her there. She accepted a cup of coffee from Gloria and sat down, conscious of a trembling in her knees.

In a way she was grateful Gloria had phoned last night — at least it had stopped her making a complete fool of herself. She'd come so close to telling Jon she loved him: would he have taken her home, made love to her? Or would he have been honest?

To her relief Jon picked up the razor and went back into the bedroom closing the door behind him. Julia gathered together her tattered dignity and turned to face Gloria, but before she could say anything Gloria said formally, "I was sorry about your husband's accident."

Normally Julia avoided discussing it but at least it had broken the uneasy silence between them. "Thank you. You knew Danny then?"

Gloria hesitated. It seemed to Julia she was choosing her words with care. "I was working on the desalination plant a few miles up the coast at the time. We ex-pats tend to stick together, meet at parties, that sort of thing."

"Is that how you met Jon?" She

couldn't stop herself asking the question.

Gloria sat back against the cushions, visibly relaxing. "Yes. It's good to see him again, although it's surprising what a small world engineering is at our level. I finished up in the Middle East a month back. I was on leave in Paris before my next posting to the Far East, so it was easy to step in when Paul had his accident."

Julia put down her cup and picked up her bag. "Well, there's no point in me hanging around if Mr Farrell's driving you back. No doubt I'll see you around." Her voice was tight, controlled.

"Are you ready Gloria?" Jon asked from the door.

"I'll just get my things." Gloria stood, smoothing down her pencil slim yellow skirt. Julia watched her as she disappeared into the bedroom. Gloria Fredericks might be a tough, top engineer, but she was definitely a woman as well, a woman from Jon's world, one who spoke his language.

"Why didn't you tell me where you were going last night," she rounded furiously on Jon.

"I didn't realise I had to account to you for my movements." His voice was dangerously reasonable.

"You do when it affects the job," she retorted hotly. "We're both out of the office now — and Max was livid this morning when he couldn't contact you. I got it in the neck — and I don't see why I should carry the can when you're out tom-catting!"

Jon's mouth was a hard white line. "What did you say?" he demanded ominously.

"Oh, I'm so sorry! Did I offend you? I suppose what's between you and Dr Fredericks is the real thing? Well, at least now she's here you won't have to waste your charms trying to get me into bed!" All control had gone: her voice was shrill, harsh.

Every word betrayed her feelings.

Jon took a step towards her. "Stop it Julia. You know perfectly well I don't spend my time trying to persuade you into bed — I've only taken what you've willingly offered." He was angry with her, but she could see the memory of their lovemaking softening his hard features. "If I've been at fault it's in not realising that you're still recovering from Danny's death. It isn't surprising that you're over-reacting to everything."

Now look here . . . "

"Let me finish," he over-rode her protests. "You're also being unfair to Gloria . . . "

"Fair! Don't talk to me about fair — how fair were you the first time we made love? And afterwards Jon, do you remember? You couldn't even be bothered to phone me . . . "

Jon turned away to the window. When he spoke his words were uncompromising, his body language unreadable. "I'm not going to try to explain," he began.

"There's no need for you to explain anything." Julia wrenched open the door. "It's all patently obvious to me."

She collected the car, accelerating away from the kerb with a scream of tyres, cutting into the heavy traffic like a London veteran, too angry to be intimidated even by Hyde Park Corner.

As she drove she turned the scene in the hotel room over and over in her mind; the shock of Jon strolling out of the bedroom, the intimacy between him and Gloria, the horrible knowledge she'd betrayed everything she felt about Jon when she'd lost her temper.

Well, she'd no intention of covering up for him. When she got back she'd ring the boss and tell him why she hadn't picked up Dr Fredericks, tell him whom she was with. Sir Max would draw his own conclusions — and Julia didn't give a damn.

★ ★ ★

"Mrs Leyton!" Julia saw the doorman waving at her just as the lift doors closed. She pressed the 'Hold' button and they slid open again. "Almost missed you — Sir Max's secretary phoned down five minutes ago. Can you go straight up to his office please?"

"Thanks Martin." Julia took the lift with a sinking heart. Her desire for vengeance had cooled considerably on the drive back. She'd just have to say that Gloria had made her own arrangements after all.

Sally wasn't in the outer office but Sir Max's door was open and Julia could hear him holding forth to somebody.

"Ah Julia!" he greeted her expansively when she looked round the door. "Come in, come in. Sorry you had a wasted journey. Jon was just telling me he's an old friend of Dr Fredericks." His bad temper had evaporated, whatever Jon had told him had put him in a good mood.

Jon was lounging next to Gloria on the sofa. He must have pushed the Jensen to the limit to get there first, but he looked relaxed, unruffled. He raised an eyebrow in sardonic greeting; Julia knew he'd guessed what she'd intended saying to Sir Max. The knowledge did nothing for her temper.

Through her irritation she realised Sir Max was uncharacteristically jovial, then she saw why. Dr Fredericks was obviously his sort of woman — the combination of femininity and engineering expertise was unique enough to have charmed him. If she hadn't been so fed up Julia would have found the spectacle amusing.

Julia had woken with a thumping headache, now, after the scene with Jon and the long drive she was feeling sick as well. Her neck and shoulders ached; next to Gloria Fredericks' tanned vitality she felt as limp as a rag doll.

She looked up to find Jon's steady blue gaze on her. No doubt he was making comparisons too, and just as unfavourably.

"Are you able to spare some time this afternoon to check that last specification before it goes off to the printers?" she asked him.

Her sarcastic tone penetrated to Sir Max; he turned to look beadily at his Personnel Manager. "Aren't you well Julia?" he demanded bluntly. "You look bloody awful. Take the rest of the day off, go home and go to bed. Can't have you below par: I need you one hundred percent for tomorrow."

As Sally put her head round the door and signalled to her boss he turned his attention back to Gloria. "Lunch is ready for us upstairs, we'll go up now."

Julia shut the door behind them and flopped down thankfully on the chair opposite Sally. Sir Max's assistant looked indignant. "The old so-and so! Fancy telling you how awful you look in front of . . ."

The fascinating Dr Fredericks?" supplied Julia.

"I can see Dr Fredericks isn't what you'd call a woman's woman."

"No, but she's definitely a man's

woman," Julia responded acidly. It was a relief to sit and bitch, however unfairly.

"I can imagine the stir she'd cause on a site in the middle of nowhere," Sally speculated. "All those macho blokes in hard hats . . . can you picture that figure in a boiler suit?"

"Only too well!"

"I wonder if Lady Faulkner would expect me to go in and chaperone them," the other girl joked.

The temptation to pour out the truth to Sally was almost overwhelming. They'd been friends a long time, and after he'd dropped her she'd suspected Sally had guessed something about her and Jon. But this wasn't the place for confidences, and after that last confrontation with Jon she was in no state to talk things over coherently with anyone!

Her stomach was churning again. Sally looked at her with concern. "However tactlessly put, the Old Man was right. I think you ought to go home.

Do you want me to get someone to drive you?"

"No, it's OK." Suddenly she wanted to be home and alone more than anything else in the world.

Driving through the leafy lanes Julia wondered if it would help to confide in Sally or talk to Meg again. She badly needed someone to help her sort out her feelings about Jon, get a sense of perspective.

No, there was no one she could face talking to. Julia put the car in the garage and shut the door. If the neighbours saw it in the drive someone might call and she was in no mood for small talk.

Julia shivered, the queasiness returning. Perhaps she'd got a bug or some sort of summer flu, which would explain why she felt so shaky. Dropping her briefcase on the kitchen counter she opened a cupboard in search of aspirin and saw the date marked on the wall calendar. Of course! That was all it was! The familiar cramp clenched her stomach as she shook out three tablets and ran a glass of water.

Then the sudden implication of her heedlessness hit her and she sat down with a bump at the kitchen table. She'd slept with Jon without a thought for the consequences . . . if things looked bad now, they *could* have been considerably worse.

She tried to imagine breaking the news to Jon she was expecting his child. No doubt he would have told her that a baby was her problem, not his. After all, he was the one who'd informed her what she did with her body was her own responsibility.

But relief was tinged with regret; if Jon had loved her nothing would have made her happier than to discover she was carrying his child. The feeling was no surprise. In discovering she loved Jon she had also discovered she wanted children. It had been Danny's clinching argument. Danny would have been a wonderful father; hopeless at nappy changing but full of fun and energy to lavish on the child. The thought was painful.

Very chastened, Julia filled a hot-water bottle and went to bed. As she fell asleep she resolved to start thinking with her head, not with her emotions — or her body.

8

"ARE we all agreed then?" Julia looked at the faces round the table. "In that case I suggest before we go on to discuss the timing of the key advertisements we break for coffee." There was a chorus of assent from the ten people present.

Julia pressed the buzzer and when Angela opened the door, mouthed, "Coffee please." She was relieved to see the rest of the group beginning to chat together. Many of them were from firms who had been rivals for big contracts in the past. It was vitally important for the success of the consortium that staff at all levels got on.

Surreptitiously Julia shook two aspirins into the palm of her hand; she had the nagging low backache she experienced every month and despite sleeping like a log the night before she still felt weary.

Jon's brooding presence across the table didn't help. She kept looking up to find his eyes on her; twice it had caused her to falter in the middle of a complicated sentence. Why was he looking at her with such concentration? Didn't he think she could cope with the meeting?

Angela wheeled in the coffee trolley; people began to gravitate towards it, breaking the formality of the meeting. Angela, knowing what was wrong, took Julia a cup and a glass of water to take the aspirin with.

"How are you feeling?" she whispered sympathetically.

"Worse then I look, I hope," Julia murmured back wryly. She'd taken extra care with her make-up that morning and worn the cobalt blue silky jumper suit she knew brought out the red in her hair. The result was deceptively vibrant.

"Have you got everything you need then?" Angela gestured towards the table.

"Thanks," Julia nodded. "You'd better get back to that report." She checked her watch and groaned inwardly. At least another hour and a half before they completed the agenda.

When she looked up again Jon was at her side, hunkering down so he could talk to her quietly.

"Are you OK?"

"Perfectly, thank you."

"Are you sure? You're as white as a sheet. Look, I'll take over the meeting if you're not up to it," he persisted.

So that was what he was worried about, whether the meeting would run smoothly! Julia looked him full in the face and lowered her voice to a fierce whisper. "Yes, everything's perfectly normal — and you can thank your lucky stars it is!" She saw the blank incomprehension on his face. "Or were you looking forward to fatherhood?"

It rocked him back on his heels. For once Julia had the satisfaction of denting his imperturbable composure.

It never crossed my mind you

might . . . I assumed you were . . . "

"You've assumed an awful lot, Jon Farrell," she whispered vehemently. "Go away and leave me alone."

"Julia," he urged, his face close to hers, "we can't leave it like this, we've got to talk. Can I come round this evening?"

"We've nothing to discuss — now or ever. Just go back to your seat and let me concentrate on this meeting!"

The other group members were already taking their places, consulting papers for the next item on the agenda. Jon had no choice but to comply.

"Right," said Julia brightly. "Advertising . . . "

The meeting wound up mid-afternoon, amid a general feeling that a great deal had been achieved. Julia stood by the door, saying goodbye to her new colleagues, glad to be on her feet after such a long time sitting down.

Julia started to tidy her desk: it wasn't yet four but she felt today she deserved to go home early.

"Where do you think you're going?" Jon demanded.

"Taking a few hours in lieu of all the overtime I've done, if that's all right with you."

"No it is not. Come and sit down, I told you we need to talk. You can't just walk out on me like this."

This was the last thing she wanted. Why hadn't she kept quiet? With a heavy sigh she sat down opposite him, kicking off her shoes and curling up in the chair. "Well?"

"For heaven's sake Julia!" He ran a hand through his hair in exasperation. "Don't you realise you've thrown me a bombshell!"

"I don't think you can have heard me properly Jon, there's nothing to worry about. I said I wasn't pregnant, not that I was."

He leapt to his feet. "As far as I'm concerned it amounts to the same thing."

"Oh Jon! I can assure you it's not!"

He ignored her laughter, deadly

serious as he towered over her. "That's not what I mean and you know it." Jon knelt down by her chair and took her hands in his. "I made love to you without even thinking of the consequences. I don't know how I could have been so irresponsible."

Jon's hands over hers were comforting, his eyes warm. More than anything else Julia wanted to be held, comforted, cuddled. Suddenly her resistance crumbled.

"Hold me Jon. I'm so tired, so tired of fighting everything."

He didn't ask her to explain, just took her in his arms and held her tightly on his lap, letting her snuggle against his chest, her hair stirring under his breath.

His shirt was cool against her cheek, his chest under it comfortingly firm, rising and falling with his steady breathing. Why, when they could be like this, did they spend so much time at loggerheads, Julia wondered despairingly. As if reading her thoughts

Jon stiffened and she was instantly alert.

"Jon what are you thinking about?" she asked softly.

"I was cursing myself for a fool, after all I'm not a schoolboy. If you must know, I suppose I assumed you were on the Pill."

"Why on earth should I be?" Julia demanded.

"Drew Scott . . ." he began fatally. It was enough, she was off his lap in an instant, hazel eyes hurt and accusing.

"You thought I was sleeping with Drew and so I was on the Pill!" she stormed. "That's why you didn't need to worry about the consequences! How very convenient!"

"I know you didn't sleep with Scott that night," he yelled back at her, appalled by his clumsiness.

Only because you saw the blankets downstairs, not because you believed me when I told you I didn't!"

"I keep telling you — who you sleep with is your affair!"

"Oh I see," she said sweetly, hands on hips, "in the same way as you sleeping with Gloria Fredericks is your affair? Well, let me tell you, however free and easy you may be I have different standards. If you want her, stay out of my life."

Jon was on his feet now, grasping her shoulders, shaking her. "You know nothing about Gloria Fredericks!"

"I can believe the evidence of my own eyes, and when I see a half-dressed man coming out of a woman's hotel bedroom I draw my own conclusions.

Suddenly there was so much anger in his eyes she was frightened. "Take your hands off me! Don't ever touch me again."

Jon let go of her as if he'd been burnt. "Then there's no point in continuing this. For some reason you never believe what I tell you. You've never believed I only want what's best for you. That hurts Julia, and I've had enough. I'm not made of stone." His back rigid he walked out.

Angela ventured her head cautiously round the office door. "Er . . . is everything all right?" she asked.

"Perfect," Julia responded drily, "A perfect end to a perfect week."

Angela looked puzzled. "But's it's only Wednesday."

"Exactly! Oh well, let's look on the bright side — things can only get better . . . "

★ ★ ★

At ten o'clock on Thursday morning Jon's desk was still unoccupied. Every time the door opened Julia expected to see him there. She was determined to be cool, completely professional, to demonstrate to Jon that she could still work with him.

At eleven it occurred to her he was doing it on purpose, keeping her on tenterhooks to give him the upper hand. She punched the button on the intercom. "Angela, did Mr Farrell say when he'd be in today?"

"Sorry, I assumed he'd left you a note. He went up to see Sir Max almost as soon as he came in this morning."

Her heart plummeted, surely she hadn't pushed Jon so far he'd gone to Sir Max and told him he wouldn't work with Julia any more, given him chapter and verse . . . no, even at his angriest he wouldn't do that to her. Would he?

She rang Sally, hoping the other girl couldn't detect her apprehension. "Sally, is Jon Farrell still with the boss?"

"Good grief no! He was only in ten minutes."

"I suppose it was too much to hope he'd tell me where he was going. We've a pile of work here."

"I shouldn't count on seeing him today or much at all this week come to that. Sir Max asked him to show the lovely Dr Fredericks round some of our sites."

"Don't tell me, I bet Max had to

184

really twist his arm to get him agree to that," said Julia tartly.

"Well, he didn't seem exactly heartbroken at the prospect," Sally concurred. "But look at it this way, if she's playing engineers with Jon Farrell, she's not in our hair."

"Has she been getting to you too?"

"As I was going home last night, she sauntered in wearing several hundred pounds worth of leather and cashmere — her idea of casual wear I presume — dumped a load of papers on my desk and announced she'd pick up the photocopies in fifteen minutes . . . "

Julia could imagine the confrontation. "What did you say?"

"I told her briefly, succinctly and very, very politely that I was not her secretary and that I would get her a temp from the typing-pool. She looked me up and down, then agreed. I was left with the definite impression I wasn't worth arguing with."

"It must have been maddening,"

Julia sympathised.

"It was, even more so because it's based on perfectly irrational jealousy! But the temptation to clock her one with the typewriter was pretty strong I must admit!"

"Be realistic Sally — she'd make mincemeat of you!"

Sally laughed. "That occurred to me. She's nearly as tall as Jon. Had you noticed?"

Julia preferred not to think about it. "If he's disappeared for the rest of the day I better get on with some work. See you Sally."

So, he was spending the rest of the week with Gloria Fredericks . . . somehow it had never occurred to Julia she'd be staying on so long. A fresh stab of jealousy shot through Julia. What did Jon see in Gloria? Julia smiled wryly as she answered her own question: what he saw was a stunning, intelligent independent woman. But why, out of all the engineers in the world, did Gloria have to pick on the one Julia loved . . . ?

There was no shortage of work but it was more routine now the pressure was off. Julia worked conscientiously, but the afternoon dragged. She was just packing up to go home when the door opened and he came in. His jeans were mud stained and he was still carrying the white hard hat which was obligatory on site.

He looked windswept, healthy, his hair blown into the casual mane she always associated with him, his colour high and his eyes bright from a day spent in his element. Julia met his gaze and all the love she'd been trying to conceal flooded through her.

Something must have shown in her eyes because he took a step towards her, his own expression questioning. "Sally told me you needed me." He looked at his own empty desk and her now clear in-tray. "So where's all this work you can't cope with?"

"I never said I couldn't cope, I merely said I was annoyed you'd cleared off for the day without even the manners to tell me you were leaving me with all the work,"

"Come on Julia, you don't need me here all day every day now the technical specifications are out of the way!" He put his hands on his hips, his exasperation evident. "I don't understand you, you made it plain you didn't want me here in the first place, now when I get out and leave you to it, that doesn't suit you either."

"I still think I had a right to know where you were going." Julia knew she was sounding petulant. "What if something urgent had come up and you were clambering round in the mud with that woman . . . "

"Oh so that's what all this about," he drawled, putting down his hard hat and sitting on the corner of the desk. "You object to me working with 'that woman'."

"Who you *work* with is your own business."

"So is who I sleep with, Julia," he drawled softly, his eyes moving over her flushed face.

There was no answer she was prepared to make to that. Without meeting his eyes Julia picked up her briefcase and swept out of the office.

At home she took down Danny's photo from the mantelpiece and tried to find some help in it. His laughing, open face gave nothing away, told her nothing new. His dark eyes were frank and amused, the eyes of a man who took nothing seriously. It was part of his charm, one of the things she'd found so attractive in him.

"You could have explained Jon to me," she said out loud, "but it was the one thing I could never ask you."

* * *

The following morning Julia bumped into Jon and Dr Fredericks in the foyer at Faulkner's. They were dressed for the site, Gloria looking just as good

189

in coveralls as Julia had guessed she would.

Julia gritted her teeth and made herself smile, despite Jon's stony expression. "Good morning Dr Fredericks, Jon."

"Good morning," Gloria stopped, ignoring Jon's obvious desire to get on. "I can see you're feeling better. I'm sorry you were dragged up to London when you weren't feeling very well."

"Oh, it was just a migraine. And driving in London's always stressful. I hope you're enjoying your visit despite having to cut short your Paris trip."

"Thanks. Everyone here's real friendly and Jon's looking after me very well." Gloria flashed him a smile. He smiled thinly in return, his eyes on Julia.

"I'm sure he is," Julia responded warmly, "I wouldn't expect anything else of him." She was rewarded with a flash of annoyance, quickly masked, then Jon said,

We must go Gloria, we've a tight schedule."

Sally was right, they were very much

of a height, Julia thought, watching him shouldering open the door for the American engineer. They made a striking couple with their tall blond good looks. Whatever that encounter had achieved, at least she'd kept her cool, not given Jon any further reason to suspect she was jealous. And she had the satisfaction of knowing she looked good too. She'd dressed with particular care that morning in a new black linen suit, cinched at the waist with a bronze sash to match her high heels.

★ ★ ★

Cleaning the house from top to bottom on Saturday was therapeutic, kept her mind off Gloria Fredericks, even off Jon. She sat down with a cup of tea and found herself gazing at Danny's photograph on the mantelpiece. With a jolt she remembered she was still no further towards understanding why he'd wanted to change jobs.

She'd got so involved with Jon, and the work for the new consortium she still hadn't got to the bottom of what must have been troubling Danny, making him want to leave the company he'd been with virtually his whole working life.

Julia felt guiltily as though she'd let him down. She'd been convinced all along she was getting the best of the bargain their marriage had been, but now . . . she knew she owed it to him to find out what had been unsettling him.

The only person who held the answer, who could explain Danny to her, was Jon. She had to go to him and ask straight out why Danny was leaving Faulkner's.

Julia showered and washed the dust out of her hair, then pulled on clean jeans and sweatshirt. Having made the decision, she needed to get it over with, and if that meant going without make-up and with her wet hair in a pony-tail, so much the better. She didn't want

Jon thinking she'd made a special effort for him.

The car-park at the boatyard was surprisingly full, but she managed to squeeze between Jon's Jensen and a large Renault. As she passed the bank manager's boat Julia realised why, a party was beginning to warm up. She smiled at the sight of so many weekend sailors in their peaked caps and brass-buttoned blazers pouring gin and tonics on deck.

The curtains were drawn and the front door was closed but there was a light on in the saloon of Jon's boat. Her soft-soled shoes made no sound on deck, besides she doubted if he'd be able to hear anything above the sound of James Last belting out from next door. Julia hesitated, suddenly unsure of the wisdom of being there; the drawn curtains gave the impression of an intimacy she was afraid of breaking.

Behind her the music reached a crashing crescendo then stopped. In the near silence she heard Jon's voice coming from the front of the boat.

The logical thing, of course, was just to turn round and go, come back another day when he was alone. The music began again, Frank Sinatra crooning a love song. Obviously the mood had mellowed Julia thought wryly, at least she could hear herself think now.

"I still don't understand why Danny had to marry her." Gloria's voice carried clearly over the water.

Jon's reply was inaudible over the music, but his tone was placatory. Julia moved forward, her soft-soled shoes soundless on the decking and crouched against the curve of the window.

"I'm not upset any more Jon, I'm good and mad. I've gotten over the shock — but the more I think about it, the madder I get. OK, I wouldn't marry him — but I never made any bones about my career being the most important thing in my life. I loved him, but I didn't want to be tied down. Hell, he even wanted kids. Can you imagine me, stuck at home with kids?"

"No," Jon replied drily.

Danny? Danny had wanted to marry *Gloria*? Had married her, Julia, on the rebound? Why hadn't he said anything to her? She'd been honest with him about Jon. Julia swallowed hard against the rising gall at the back of her throat. She'd wanted to know what was troubling Danny, now she did she'd have given anything not to have heard.

"I was prepared for him to end our affair when I wouldn't marry him, but when he came back from Europe nothing had changed. Admitted, he never mentioned marriage again but I assumed he'd accepted my terms. Then I fly in to London, and the first thing I know you're telling me he'd gotten himself a wife!"

Julia felt dizzy. Danny had been unfaithful to her, *her husband* had been unfaithful to her. Not casually, yielding to a moment's temptation through loneliness, but deliberately, repeatedly, cold-bloodedly. He'd set up a home and acquired a wife to go in it, and then returned to his mistress. Everything she'd believed about Danny, his honesty with her, his integrity was shattered, even his image seemed clouded in her mind.

Jon's reply was indistinct, then Gloria spoke sharply, her strong voice clear over the water. "I don't want to listen to you defending him Jon. He was a bastard, and I should have known better. Let me tell you who I feel sorry for right now, and that's the kid he married. I hope to heaven she never finds out about this!"

"She'll never hear it from me," Jon's voice was hard.

"I'm sure she won't! You knew — but you never told me until you were forced to. You men make me sick the way you stick together." Gloria's voice was rising with her gathering anger. Despite her own pain Julia heard the anguish, realised Gloria had really loved Danny.

"Calm down," Jon began.

"No! I'm going!" There was a clatter as a chair hit the deck. "I thought you were on my side, but you're the pits Jon Farrell, and so was Danny."

Julia saw the other woman jump to the tow-path and run past too upset to notice the crouched figure on deck.

"Hell and damnation," Jon swore violently. He stood and turned, coming face to face with Julia painfully straightening from her miserable huddle on the gunwale.

9

"**W**HAT are you doing here? Did you hear all that?" Jon demanded. Under the tan his skin was grey, the hard lines round his mouth sharply defined — by anger, or by the shock of finding her there, Julia was too dazed to wonder or care which. She nodded dully, letting him shepherd her into the saloon.

Jon slammed the doors against the row of the party next door, then pushed her none too gently into a chair.

"We both need a drink." He handed her a tumbler with a generous measure of whisky. "Get it down, it'll help."

Obediently Julia gulped the fiery liquid, shuddering as it burnt its way to her stomach. She looked sideways at Jon. "Is it true?" she whispered.

"Yes." He took another drink, his eyes fixed on her face.

"At least now you're being honest with me. Why didn't you tell me before?"

"Would you really have wanted to know? You didn't suspect anything." He paused, then added with a shadow of his old mockery, "Any way would you have believed me?"

The shot went home. "*That* was what you were hinting at the day you came back. Why didn't you say, instead of making vague insinuations?"

"I tried to. But you wouldn't listen."

"Can you blame me after the way you'd behaved? And the way you've shielded Danny only proves I was right! I trusted him," she whispered. "That trust was really important to me."

"You don't understand. I tried to explain to Gloria. Danny was capable of living his life in compartments. You were in the compartment labelled 'wife'."

Julia stared at him uncomprehendingly. "How can you be so cynical? How can you live like that?"

"I can't," Jon responded, "but Danny could."

"If he had her why did he want me too?" Julia was struggling to make sense of this new image of her husband.

"Because you're beautiful, intelligent, independent," Jon catalogued flatly, his eyes fixed on the amber liquid in his glass. "He'd arrived at a point in his life where he needed roots, when he needed someone to come home to. Gloria wouldn't give him that. You fitted the bill very well."

She could accept the fact that Danny had married her because he couldn't have Gloria, in the way she had married him because she couldn't have Jon. He had never pretended it was a love match between them. But how could he have carried on, resumed his relationship with Gloria, as if nothing had changed, when he had a wife he'd sworn to be faithful to?

"It doesn't mean he didn't love you," Jon was suddenly vehement. "But he loved you in one way and he loved Gloria in another. He wasn't monogamous, but he was romantic enough to believe he was being faithful to both of you. He'd never willingly have hurt you Julia."

"I can't forgive him!" she burst out passionately.

Jon's eyes captured and held hers. "And you . . . are you so sure your motives for marrying him were so pure?"

"If you mean I went to him on the rebound from you, that's true," Julia was stung into honesty. "He was kind to me, gave me back my self-respect after you'd thrown it in my face. And don't try and put me in the wrong to make you feel better about condoning his behaviour. Gloria was right, the male mafia sticks together. Did you sit together laughing at our gullibility? How cosy."

All at once Jon lost his temper, slamming his glass at the wall, shattering it in a spray of glass and pungent liquid. Then, before she knew what was happening, he was across the room, dragging her to her feet.

"Damn it woman! Why don't you ever listen to what I say? I never once said I condoned what Danny had done, all I was trying to do was explain to you how his mind worked, hoping it would make it less painful. Do you think I went racing up to London to break the news about you to Gloria because I enjoyed the experience? She's a friend: I've never laid a finger on her, but I'm sure you won't believe that."

His fingers tightened painfully on her wrist. "I'd spent months supporting Gloria after Danny was killed, lying, hiding your existence from her. And then to have to tell her about you, ask her to cover up her own hurt for your sake — I think she did a damn good job.

"Do you really believe I spent weeks after the accident covering up the gossip out of some feeling of male solidarity, ignoring telexes from Max demanding to know why I was still in the Middle

East? I did it for you, to try and save you pain." He shook her, his eyes almost black with the intensity of his feelings. "I might as well have saved myself the trouble."

Jon released her and turned away, the flash-flood of anger ebbing as quickly as it had come. "I need a drink. What the devil did I do with that glass?"

"You . . . broke it," Julia faltered. He'd done all that for her, and she'd paid him back by throwing it in his face. Now she could never tell him she loved him.

Julia wrenched open the saloon door and was met by the impact of the party in full swing. A wall of sound and blurred, shifting colour hit her senses: shrieks of laughter, tinkling glasses, conversation shouted over the insistent thump of the stereo.

Jon's arm snaked round her waist, pulling her bodily back into the saloon. He kicked the door to and released her. "You can't leave in that state — and you certainly can't drive."

"Let me go Jon . . . just because you don't want your neighbours to see me . . . " Stubbornly she kept her chin down, scuffing the carpet with her toe, aware she was behaving badly but unable to stop herself. After the high drama of the last half-hour this was a ludicrous anticlimax. She had no idea how to behave to Jon after everything they'd said.

"You look like a tomboy caught pinching apples!" Jon seemed amused despite himself. "Come here, you're not safe out!"

Indignant, Julia raised her eyes to wither him with a look and found herself enfolded, held against his chest. Even after all the anger between them it felt right, safe to be there, like coming home after an arduous journey.

Under her cheek his fast breathing was the last vestige of his anger. Through the thin shirt she felt the tautness in his body gradually relax as the adrenalin drained away. She let herself relax with him, but warily.

She'd never seen Jon lose his temper like that before.

Jon gently disentangled himself. "You look about twelve. It must be the effect of the red nose." He handed her his handkerchief. "Here, stop sniffing."

Julia blew her nose and stuffed the hanky in her jeans pocket. "Thanks for the compliment," she retorted. "You're a real morale booster."

"Well, if I'm nice to you you'll only weep all over me," he said. "And this is my last clean shirt." It was there again, the laughter in his voice.

"I'd better get a dustpan and a brush and pick up that broken glass before one of us steps on it." Julia headed for the galley, glad for something to do.

Jon raked his fingers through his hair looking round incredulously at the mess. "I really blew my top, didn't I?"

"There's no need to sound so apologetic about it," Julia dropped the larger fragments into the dustpan. "I gave you enough provocation."

He knelt down beside her and gingerly picked out the finer shards from the weave. "It wasn't just you, Gloria took it out on me too."

"Then there really never was anything between the two of you?"

"Other than friendship, no."

"I got the feeling you weren't exactly immune to her good looks," Julia suggested slyly.

"She's not my type but . . . "

"There's nothing wrong with your hormones?" Despite her jealousy she was amused at his reaction.

"What are you grinning about?" Jon demanded, taking the brush from her.

Julia shook her head. It was nothing really, just a great relief that the anger between them had gone.

He wrapped the broken glass in newspaper and dumped it in the pedal bin. "I'm starving. Have you eaten?"

She hadn't, she'd been in too much of a hurry to see Jon while she still had the impetus, and she hadn't eaten since lunch. It was now nine o'clock.

"No, I'm starving too. Shall I cook something? What's in the fridge?"

"Plenty, but it's all going to take too long. Fancy a take-away?"

"Yes please. Chinese, with lots of spare ribs . . . and special fried rice . . . and spring rolls . . . "

"OK," Jon grinned, "I get the message, you're hungry." He picked up his wallet from the bureau, stuffing it in the back pocket of his jeans. "Set the table and put the plates in the oven, I'll be back in fifteen minutes. There's some cider in the bottom cupboard."

Julia had found the plates and put the oven on low before the incongruity of the situation struck her. Here she was, calmly preparing for a meal, and half an hour before she'd been told by the man she loved that her husband had been unfaithful to her throughout their marriage.

How could she accept it so easily? She knew Jon was telling her the truth, there was no possibility of misunderstanding him. She should be shattered, but somehow she felt strangely calm.

Julia pulled out drawers searching for cutlery and napkins, hands working mechanically, setting the table.

"Are the plates hot?" Jon pushed through the door, his hands full of small carrier bags.

Julia jumped, so engrossed in her thoughts she hadn't heard him return. Jon started to open the packages.

"How many people are eating this lot?"

"Just you and me — unless you've invited someone else. I'll call the James Last Appreciation Society from next door if you feel we can't cope."

"You won't! Julia forked out a large portion of rice. "Did you remember the spare ribs?"

"Carnivore!" Jon grinned. "I asked for double — leave some for me."

The storm of emotion had left them both ravenous. Neither spoke until the table was littered with empty foil cartons.

"Do you want the last spring roll?" Jon offered.

"I'm so full I'll never eat again," Julia groaned. "You have it."

"We'll save it for the swans tomorrow. They'll probably appreciate it after all the crisps and dry roast peanuts they'll have been fed this evening."

"How much longer is that racket going to go on next door?"

"Judging by the last time they threw a party, about 2 a.m. I wish they'd change the record though." Jon swept the debris into the carrier bags and stacked their plates in the sink. "I'll put the kettle on, we can drink our coffee in the bedroom, it'll be slightly more peaceful."

In spite of the casualness of his remark Julia stiffened. The one complication she didn't need right now was to find herself in Jon's bedroom! But why should she assume he had ulterior motives? It was about time she learned to trust him, and herself.

A glance in the bathroom mirror

reassured her. Her nose was no longer red — that remark had really rankled! — but she looked as scrubbed and innocent as the tomboy he'd called her, and about as alluring. She'd hardly send his pulses racing looking this way.

Jon had evidently taken her agreement for granted, there was no sign of him in the saloon. She pushed open the door with trepidation: he was sitting propped up against the pillows, his long legs stretched out.

"Coffee's on the chest of drawers. Guests get to sit in the chair." He gestured at a rickety basket chair by the side of the bed.

Julia sat down gingerly and sipped her coffee, conversation deserting her. What could you say to a man while sitting in a room which evoked such intimate memories? Last time she'd been there she had been in his arms, almost in his bed. Then their bodies had done the talking . . .

Before she could stop herself her eyes

210

travelled up his lean frame. She looked up with a jerk to find him scrutinising her in turn.

"How do you feel now?"

"Fine, I was really hungry. Did you go to the Chinese restaurant in the village?"

"That's not what I meant," he responded evenly. Despite his relaxed pose, head thrown back against the pillows, he was watching her minutely. "You've had a bad shock. Have you really taken in what I told you about Danny? Because if there's anything else, let's get it out of the way now."

"Only one thing. Danny's briefcase — what was in it you didn't want me to see?"

Jon smiled thinly. "Just details about the Far East job — and the flat he was planning to buy with Gloria in Kuala Lumpur."

The final pieces fell into place. Julia swallowed hard.

"You did a lot to save me pain Jon, and all I did was mistrust you. I'm sorry. I was finding things out about myself as well as about Danny . . . " *and my love for you*, but that was the one thing she couldn't say to him.

He was still watching her face intently. "I must say you're taking this better than I expected Julia. Are you sure it's all sunk in? Get this out of your system now, or it'll ruin your life."

She spoke slowly, working it out aloud as much for her own sake as for Jon's. "I've mourned for Danny. I accept now there was someone else the whole time, but . . . " she looked Jon straight in the eye, "it may be shock, I may feel differently tomorrow, but right now, I believe you . . . I do believe, in his own way, he thought he was being faithful to me."

"I know that," Jon spoke so quietly she had to strain to hear him.

"And you were right about one thing: my own motives for marrying him were . . . open to question. But he knew about us, and accepted it. I really intended to be a good wife to him. I really believed it would work."

"Danny could be very persuasive."

Suddenly Julia had had enough. "I want to go home, I want to go to bed, I just want to sleep."

"Stay here." It wasn't an invitation and it wasn't an order, but fell somewhere between the two.

"Jon, I can't . . ." Julia whispered, uncertain what she was refusing.

"I don't want you driving, and after what's happened I don't think you should be by yourself tonight." He got off the bed. "You have the bed, I'll bunk down on the couch."

She hadn't the energy to refuse him. "OK. Thanks Jon." The thought of not having to return to the empty house, the big empty double bed, was overwhelmingly attractive.

"Can you find me something to sleep in? An old shirt will do."

"I can do better than that." With a flourish he produced a pair of blue and white striped pyjamas from the chest of drawers.

"Jon! You never wear those!"

"Christmas present from my grandmother, to keep me warm in damp foreign beds! " He laughed. "I don't think this is quite what she had in mind, but you take the top and I'll have the bottoms. There's a new toothbrush in the bathroom cabinet. Is there anything else you need?"

"No, I don't think so." As he turned to go Julia put out one hand and touched him shyly. "Thanks Jon . . . I . . . I didn't want to be alone tonight."

Jon smiled briefly, touched her cheek in a fleeting caress and carrying a blanket and pillow went into the saloon.

Her own pillow was redolent of Jon's aftershave. Julia snuggled her face into it, curling into a ball, then stretching out until the tips of her toes touched the bed-end.

She never imagined she'd be sleeping on the boat tonight, be here in Jon's bed — alone. The picture of his long, relaxed body stretched out down the length of it came into her mind and with it something which hadn't occurred to her when she'd accepted his offer. He was a tall man, at least six foot two, and the couch would be uncomfortably short. If he was going to get any sleep it would have to be on the floor.

Julia hopped out of bed and into the saloon before she had time to think about what she was doing. Jon was rolled in the blanket on the floor, pummelling the pillow in an attempt to get comfortable.

"What's the matter?"

"This is ridiculous Jon, you can't sleep on the floor. Let's do a swap. I'll take the couch, I'm short enough. You go back to bed. At least that way we'll both get some rest.

"That couch is bloody uncomfortable," he said with feeling, "and the racket coming from next door is enough to wake the dead. We'll share the bed."

He freed himself from the blanket and stood up. The pyjama bottoms rested snugly on his hips, their unattractiveness doing nothing to hide the fact that here was a very sexy man.

Julia swallowed hard, and shook her head. "Jon, we can't . . . it wouldn't be sensible."

"I haven't forgotten what you told me the other day. And I haven't forgiven myself for being so thoughtless. When I say sleep I mean just that Julia, nothing else, I promise."

Julia believed him. She turned and padded barefoot back to bed followed by Jon.

"What side do you want?"

Julia dithered by the side of the bed. In a crazy way this was worse, more intimate than when they'd made love, because it was so ordinary. There was no fever sweeping them along, only kindness and friendship and these were unfamiliar qualities in their relationship recently.

"Stop dithering there like a virgin on your wedding night." he laughed, "and get in!"

"Jon!" she protested, scrambling into the left-hand side of the bed.

In the moment before he switched off the light she saw his teeth flash in a huge grin. "Do you prefer tea or coffee in the morning? What a lot of things I don't know about you." His voice was suddenly husky. He put one arm around her shoulders, pulling her into the shelter of his body, so her cheek rested against the flat plane of his chest.

She went to him without resistance, moulding her body down the warm length of his flank, listening to his breathing slow as he drifted off to sleep.

Julia wasn't aware of falling asleep, only of waking to find Jon beside her. She lay with her eyes closed listening to the unfamiliar sounds of the early morning river; water slapping gently against the boat, the comic pinging call of the coots. They'd moved apart in the night, but he was close enough for her to feel his warmth beside her, his very stillness a sign of how deeply he slept.

If only this moment could last forever. This was what she'd always wanted, to be here lying beside the man she loved, secure, without any misunderstandings.

Afraid to break the spell she slowly opened her eyes. Jon was lying with his face turned towards her, so close she could see the laughter lines drawn on the fine skin around his eyes. The strong expressive lips were relaxed in a half smile, dark blond stubble already shadowing his upper lip.

She wanted to put out a finger to trace the sharply chiselled line of his mouth, but she stopped herself just in time. If she woke him with a caress, while he was still drugged with sleep, his response would be automatic, ruining the fragile trust between them. If they made love she'd never be able to hide her feelings for him again, and however kind he'd been last night he hadn't mentioned love. How could he, when he didn't love her?

Julia remembered the look that had passed between them that evening in the office. If he woke now and looked at her like that again she'd have to tell him how she felt.

As she thought it Jon opened his eyes, staring into hers with wary wakefulness. "Good morning, did you sleep well?" His tone was perfectly friendly, he could have been greeting her at work. Anything less romantic was difficult to imagine, but at least it solved the problem of how to react to him.

"Very well thank you." Her voice was equally non-committal.

"You never told me . . . " He was out of bed, pulling on a sweatshirt.

"Told you what?" she asked, suddenly short of breath.

"Whether you prefer tea or coffee first thing," he finished.

Was that all? "Tea please."

219

Julia went to the bathroom, stripped off and washed quickly. She released her hair from the ribbon, shaking it loose with a mutter of annoyance as she saw the kink that had dried in. There was a bottle of *Chanel for Men* in the bathroom cabinet; a dab of that behind the ears would wake her up. She slipped the pyjama top on again and got back into bed just as Jon came in carrying a tray and the Sunday papers. He passed her a cup and settled down to read in companionable silence.

Julia ate toast and flicked through the colour supplement, scanning the articles without seeing them, acutely aware of Jon next to her in the bed. What did he expect her to do? As a social situation it was beyond her experience; did he expect her to stay for lunch or should she get up and thank him politely for the use of his bed? Eventually she put down the magazine and cleared her throat.

"Er . . . Jon . . . I don't know quite

how to put this . . . "

"But where do we go from here?" he interrupted. "We can't pretend things haven't changed between us now you know the truth about Danny, now I don't have to hide it from you. I'd like to go on seeing you Julia, now we've cleared the air. We're older, wiser than we were before." He took her hand, his voice more urgent. "Things can be different. But I'll be off to Brazil soon . . ."

"And all we'd have is a part-time relationship? I've had enough of that Jon," she said bitterly.

"It needn't be like that for us," he protested.

"It would be exactly like that for us, with the possible exception that, unlike Danny, you might be faithful to me — for a while. Or were you proposing an open relationship?"

She knew her unhappiness was distorting her face but it would hurt more having him like that than not having him at all. And how could she conceal her love for him? It would be like the first time all over again — he'd run from the first signs of emotional commitment, probably accuse her of nest-building.

Well it wasn't enough, she'd rather live without Jon, build a life of her own, than be dependent on the crumbs that dropped from his table.

"It's not enough Jon, I'm sorry, but I want to be independent. I'm free of the past, the last thing I want to do is start all that again."

Julia threw back the sheet, picked up her clothes and went into the bathroom to get dressed. When she emerged Jon hadn't moved. "Goodbye Jon," she said from the doorway.

"Goodbye, if that's what you want." His eyes were shuttered.

"I'm very grateful," she began.

Jon sat up with a jerk, his face working with anger. "I don't want your gratitude," he snarled.

Julia spun on her heel and ran.

* * *

Julia was conscious of George her next door neighbour on the other side of the hedge that divided their two gardens but she ignored him, in no mood for neighbourly banter. She clipped at the beech twigs with the secateurs feeling a savage satisfaction every time the blades met and another sprig fell to the lawn.

The way she felt at the moment if she never spoke to another man again, it would be too soon. Her shock at Jon's revelations about Danny had crystallised into anger. She'd told Jon she understood but forgiving was harder. It wasn't enough to say Danny hadn't been a one-woman man: he'd made promises at the altar he'd never had any intention of keeping.

Julia raked up the clippings, heaped them into the wheelbarrow and pushed it over the bare patch of earth, a pity she couldn't tidy up her life as easily as she could the garden. It was strange the only person she felt any sympathy for in the whole wretched mess was Gloria; she knew exactly how she was feeling — betrayed and humiliated.

The phone began to ring. She ran to the kitchen door, kicking off her boots before grabbing the receiver.

"Julia?" Of course, it had to be Jon! Why couldn't he leave her alone?

"Yes?"

"Come out to dinner with me tonight." It was more an order than invitation.

"No!" There was silence at the other end of the line, then Jon demanded: "Why not?"

She said the first thing that came into her head. I'm having dinner with Drew Scott." Instantly she regretted it. She should have just hung up in him.

"I see." His voice was flat and hard. "Well, I mustn't keep you then. Have a good time." He put down the receiver abruptly before she could reply.

Julia groaned. What on earth had

made her say that? Because she knew it was one thing guaranteed to rile him? But on second thoughts it might not be such a bad idea. She owed Drew something for the way she'd dropped him when she'd started to work with Jon.

Drew answered the phone immediately. "Dinner tonight? Great. Where do you want to go?"

"This is on me," Julia said firmly. "How about *Le Petit Trianon*?"

"You must take me out more often," Drew teased. "I could get used to eating like that! I'll call for you at seven thirty."

Fortunately, Julia was able to get a table. She and Danny had often eaten there and the head waiter remembered her.

She went upstairs, determined tonight she was going to look her best, not only for Drew, but for herself.

Julia knew she'd succeeded when she saw the look on his face when she opened the door that evening.

The apricot silk dress with its boned, strapless bodice and tulip skirt gave her curves she never usually exploited. She'd tonged her hair into a shining chestnut curtain and brought out the green in her eyes with skilful make-up.

"You look gorgeous," he said finally, standing back to admire the full effect. So did he; his dark good-looks emphasised by the formal dinner jacket and bow tie. It was obvious that he too had pulled out all the stops.

"Shall we have an aperitif before we go?" Julia asked. "The table's booked for eight, it's only a ten-minute drive."

★ ★ ★

"What do you think? A bottle of the '82 Claret?" Drew handed back the wine list as she nodded in agreement. "So, how have you spent your weekend?"

Julia looked at him and wondered

226

just how he'd react if she told him she'd spent the night in Jon Farrell's bed — however chastely — after discovering her husband had kept a mistress throughout their marriage.

"Gardening and cleaning," she said lightly.

"It's a big house," Drew commented. "Do you have help?"

"Yes. It didn't seem too big until I started work again. Now . . . I don't know. It's a large house for one person . . . I may sell it." It hadn't occurred to her until she said it, but it made good sense practically — and emotionally, a step free of the past. It held too many ghosts of Danny and Jon.

"Have you seen anything else you'd like to buy, or were you thinking of moving in with someone?" Drew took a sip of the red wine, then swirled it round the glass, watching her thoughtfully.

"Definitely *not* moving in with anyone else!"

Drew's eyebrows shot up at her

vehemence. "I see, sorry I asked. I assume you and Farrell have had another row."

Julia stared at him, surprised by his sharpness. "What do you mean?"

"Come off it Julia. I was surprised when you phoned me, but pleased to be seeing you again. Now I'm wondering why you asked me. You're upset about something, don't think I can't tell — and I'd lay odds it's connected with Jon Farrell. If you want cheering up, fine, but don't think you can use me to make him jealous."

Julia stared at him guiltily, recognising the truth of what he was saying. Why else had she told Jon it was Drew she was going out with? Because she knew it would get to him.

"I'm sorry Drew. You've every right to be angry. But it isn't as trivial as you make it sound." Her voice began to shake. "I discovered last night that Gloria Fredericks had been Danny's mistress all the time we were married."

"Oh my God," Drew took both her

hands in his. "Julia I'm so sorry! No wonder you needed some company, and here am I taking the top of your head off because my male ego's been dented! How did you find out?"

Julia smiled wryly, "You weren't far wrong — Jon told me."

"*Jon* told you! Why?"

"Let's say he had no choice. I know it seems I'm using you, but I really needed someone tonight."

"What the hell's Jon Farrell doing leaving you alone? I'd have thought you were close enough for him to understand how you must be feeling," Drew demanded angrily.

"That's the real problem Drew. I love him — but he doesn't love me."

"I'd like to bang your heads together!" Drew dropped her hands and sat back in exasperation. His eyes flicked to the doorway, then back to her face again. "For two intelligent people you're both acting very stupidly!"

"What?" Then Drew surprised her even more: he picked up her hand

and kissed the palm with lingering intensity.

Behind her Sir Max's voice said, "Good evening Andre, hope we've got our usual table. Good. Jon, if you and Gloria sit over there . . . "

10

"WHAT are they doing here?" Julia hissed.

"I thought you knew Jon was going to be here. I thought that was the reason you'd asked me."

"I didn't! Believe me Drew — I wouldn't use you like that. And Jon's the last person I want to see again."

"You really do love him, don't you?"

"Yes," Julia whispered, conscious of his hand still holding hers.

Drew's fingers tightened as she moved to free herself. With deliberate slowness he brought them to his lips again, meeting her eyes with a look that said. "Trust me." He relinquished his hold and raised his glass in an intimate toast to her.

Startled by this show of affection and by Jon's unexpected presence, Julia struggled to maintain her composure.

The hairs on the back of her neck prickled: Jon was staring at her, she could feel it.

"Drew, I want to go home!"

"Don't panic. We've got a perfect right to be here. It won't do Farrell any harm to see you with someone else. Anyway, the waiter's coming with our starters.

"I could probably cope with Jon, but not Gloria Fredericks as well!"

All the images she'd repressed came flooding in: Danny with Gloria . . .

"You've got to face it sometime, it may as well be now."

Julia recognised the truth of what he was saying but she still felt raw with misery. Out of the corner of her eye she saw the head waiter seating Sir Max's party at the circular central table. Jon's back was to her, but she could see Gloria clearly.

The striking American was pale and set under her tan. Julia felt a pang of fellow feeling. She wished she could get the other woman alone, talk to her.

"You're not jealous of Gloria Fredericks are you?" Drew had followed her gaze.

"Strangely enough, no. It wasn't her fault — she never knew he was a married man," Julia said. "Jon told me Danny wanted to marry her, but she refused. I always knew there was something in his past, but not that. Why couldn't he tell me? That's what hurts — I thought we'd been honest with each other."

The waiter was handing out menus at the other table. Gloria took hers without a word, her eyes still on Julia. Lady Faulkner, leaning across to speak to her saw where she was looking and waved.

"Look dear," Julia heard her say, tapping Sir Max's arm, "there's Julia and Drew!"

Sir Max twisted round in his chair, smiled and gave them a brief salute before turning back to the wine list. Lady Faulkner touched his arm again and after a few moments he rose and came across to them.

"Don't get up Drew," he pressed the

younger man back into his seat, "I just came across to ask you to join us, if we're not interrupting anything."

"That's very nice of you," she began, forcing a smile, "but we don't want to break up your party, and we've already started . . ."

"It doesn't matter darling," Drew interjected. "We can ask the waiter to hold our main course. Thank you very much sir, we'd love to." He was on his feet pulling out her chair before she could protest.

"Excellent," said Sir Max heartily, then added *sotto voce*, "actually you'll be doing Joan and I a favour. It's turning into a very sticky party. Seemed a good idea at the time, but Joan hasn't taken to Gloria Fredericks, and Jon's in a filthy temper for some reason.

Drew put his arm round Julia as they made their way to the central table. "What are you playing at?" she demanded under her breath.

"Just play along, I know what I'm doing."

The waiters were already relaying the table for the new arrivals. Sir Max seated Julia between Lady Faulkner and Jon, placing Drew between himself and Gloria. Oh perfect! thought Julia, next to Jon and under Gloria's brooding eyes . . .

"Good evening Joan," she smiled at Lady Faulkner with genuine warmth; she'd known Sir Max's wife for a long time and could imagine how she was reacting to her husband's blatant appreciation of Gloria Fredericks.

"It's wonderful to see you looking so well my dear. You've got a really healthy colour."

Yes, Julia thought, probably crimson with embarrassment. The older woman turned to Drew. "Look after her, you're a very lucky young man."

"Don't I know it Lady Faulkner."

Julia heard Jon inhale sharply. She couldn't just sit there, she'd have speak to him before the evening deteriorated into a complete shambles.

"Hello Jon, we've turned up at the

same dinner-table after all."

"So it seems," he said tightly, his eyes raking over her flushed face.

"Have you met Dr Gloria Fredericks Julia?" Joan asked. Julia caught a faint edge of desperation in the question. Lady Faulkner was not easily rattled. Forty years of marriage to Max as he worked his way up had long ago given her with the ability to cope with most situations, but it was evident that the cross-currents between the four people sharing her dinner party were stretching her to the limit.

"We've met. In fact we've got quite a lot in common." Julia looked straight at Gloria.

Colour came back to Gloria's face with a vengeance, then she shot Jon a look of sheer anger.

Joan Faulkner's expression clearly said she wished she was somewhere else! Julia felt a stab of contrition; she really ought to try to help salvage something from the evening.

"Will you be off to the Algarve this

autumn Joan?" she asked, knowing they had a villa there.

"Definitely," Sir Max interjected, "I'm not missing my golf for anything. Do you play golf Gloria?"

"No, I've never had the time." Julia guessed the effort it was costing her to make social chit-chat.

"Well you must let me give you a lesson while you're here, see if you like it. You've certainly got the shoulders for a good swing."

Joan rolled her eyes at Julia who suppressed a giggle. Jon sat in icy isolation while Julia chatted on to Joan, beginning to believe they might get through to the end of this ghastly meal after all.

Eventually she excused herself and went to the powder-room. As she reapplied her lipstick the door opened behind her and Gloria came in. Their eyes met in the mirror.

"You know," Gloria stated flatly.

Julia swivelled round to face her. "Yes. Jon."

"I suppose he couldn't resist telling you."

"It wasn't like that!" Julia found herself defending him. "I overheard you talking on the boat; he hadn't any choice."

"I didn't know Danny was married, believe me."

"I know you didn't," Julia responded quietly, recognising how difficult this was for Gloria. "We're both victims. I've got no quarrel with you."

The other woman sat down on the stool next to her. "Well," she said drily, "you're not taking this as I expected. I thought you'd be distraught. Jon led me to believe . . ."

"That I was sobbing into a glass of Scotch?"

He certainly gave me the impression you couldn't cope."

"I admit it was a shock when I found out . . . then I blamed everyone — you, Jon, myself."

"But not Danny?" her voice was quizzical. "It was always very difficult

238

to blame Danny for anything, wasn't it? That was part of his charm."

"Yes," Julia considered, "I suppose it was." She remembered the few occasions she had been mad with him, how difficult it was to sustain the anger in the face of his rueful apologies.

Gloria got to her feet. "I'm glad we've talked. I'm going back to the States tomorrow, it's unlikely we'll meet again." She met Julia's eyes in the mirror. "Are you going to be OK?"

It was strange how the two of them could be so concerned about each other. "Yes, I've got my family — and my job. You?"

Gloria shrugged off the question. "My job was always the most important thing in my life, that was the problem. But you've got to carry on working with people who knew Danny. With Jon." So Gloria had guessed. Julia dropped her eyes from that too perceptive gaze.

"I can always change my job. Come on, we'd better get back."

As they reseated themselves Julia was aware that both Jon and Drew were looking at them searchingly. She ignored Jon, giving Drew a reassuring smile. Sir Max gestured to the wine waiter, but was forestalled by Drew saying, "Let me." After a brief look at the wine list he said, "Bollinger '81."

Everyone waited in anticipation while the bottle of champagne was produced and opened, intrigued to know what had prompted Drew's extravagance. A cold knot of apprehension gripped Julia's stomach. What was he up to now?

All eyes were on the waiter at Drew's shoulder, except Jon. He turned, eyes narrowed in speculation on Julia, "What game are you playing?"

She only wished she knew but Drew appeared to be making up the rules as he went along, she'd just have to trust him.

The champagne foamed into the tall glasses, the pale straw-coloured liquid imposing its own magic on the company despite the tense atmosphere. Drew raised his glass and looked round at their expectant faces. Julia willed him to get on with it — the suspense was making her feel quite ill.

"I'd like you all to drink to someone very special to me. To Julia!"

Julia was aware of the variety of reactions around the table to Drew's toast. Her boss regarded her quizzically from under his brows. Joan whispered wickedly, "Do I hear wedding bells?"

Gloria was watching Jon intently.

Julia steeled herself to meet Jon's eyes. He was white under his tan, his skin stretched taut across his cheekbones, the harsh lines scored deep beside his mouth. "Aren't you going to drink to me too, Jon?" She was breathless, as though all the air had been squeezed from her lungs. Was this the reaction Drew had been aiming for?

He raised his champagne flute in a white-knuckled grip, but his voice was mocking. "I always wished you well Julia . . . pity you never believed me." The thin stem snapped between his fingers, spilling the wine down his shirt-front in a spreading stain. A droplet of blood fell on to the white linen tablecloth.

"Jon! You've cut yourself. Let me see." She seized his hand, trying to unclench the bent fingers. Everyone else around the table had ceased to exist, reality revolved around the taut brown fingers in hers. "Let me look!" she insisted fiercely. Suddenly he capitulated, uncurling his hand into her palm. The cut was deep, slashing the length of his middle finger.

"I think I'll go and get it stitched. If you'll excuse me Lady Faulkner, Gloria." He freed his hand, rose to go.

"Max you can't let him drive!" Joan protested.

"I'm quite all right," Jon waved Max back into his seat. "My GP lives just round the corner, I'll walk there."

Julia sat frozen remembering the

look of desolation in Jon's face in the moment before the glass had broken. What devil had prompted her to go along with Drew's playacting?

Sir Max put a restraining hand on Jon's arm as he walked past him. "Sure you're OK?"

"Sure. I've had much worse." Julia met his eyes: his expression was as empty of emotion as a desert waste.

"Are you all right Julia?" Joan sounded concerned.

"No, I feel sick," Julia admitted, getting shakily to her feet.

"The sight of blood affects me the same way," the other woman sympathised. "Drew, you better take her home at once."

Julia was scarcely aware of leaving the restaurant or of Drew sitting her in the car.

"Put your head between your knees." He commanded, pushing her shoulders down until the dark swirling ceased.

"It's not the blood," she whispered, leaning her head back against the seat.

"I know that." He turned the key in the ignition, manoeuvering out of the crowded car-park.

"What a dreadful evening."

"I don't know, I think it went rather well," Drew said judiciously. "Shame about Jon's hand though, it looked nasty."

Julia gasped. "*Rather well*! How could you be so insensitive? I must have been mad to go along with you anyway!" She was angry and she let it show.

"Let's get inside." Drew pulled up to the kerb outside her house, ignoring her furious stare as he opened the front door and ushered her into the living-room.

"Sit down, drink this," he passed her a whisky tumbler, "and listen to me."

Julia collapsed into an armchair, took a sip of the whisky with a shudder of distaste and waited. There was nothing else to do.

Drew propped an elbow on the mantelpiece. "The morning Jon turned up on your doorstep and found me in the house — you remember?"

"As if I could forget!"

"I knew the reason he'd come was to check if we'd spent the night together. And he'd only do that if he was jealous. And he'd only be jealous if he cared for you. Right?"

"Wrong Drew. He was jealous all right — but only because we . . . we were lovers once."

"I don't think you're being honest with yourself Julia. Has it occurred to you why you're always fighting?"

"Because we don't like each other!"

"Because you like each other too much! You've already told me you love him — that little charade in the restaurant was to force him to realise he's in love with you."

"No," Julia shook her head. She couldn't allow herself to believe it.

"So why did he cover up after Danny died? Don't tell me it was just out of loyalty to Danny. And it certainly wasn't for Gloria's sake — that's one

245

lady who can look after herself. I know for sure Max ordered him home and he refused to come. Who would he put his career on the line for like that?"

She couldn't bring herself to answer.

"Well?" Drew persisted, refusing to let her off the hook.

"He did it for me."

"And why should he?"

"Because he loved me." Her lips were stiff with the effort not to cry.

"Because he loves you," Drew corrected, "present tense. And because he believed you were in love with Danny and he didn't want you hurt."

"No, he can't love me any longer." Julia shook her head.

"Oh for heaven's sake! Everyone else can see it." Drew threw up his hands in exasperation. "Why can't you? Why do you think I did what I did this evening?"

"To make him jealous?"

"To force his hand. Can you sit there and tell me after the way he reacted he's not in love with you?"

"Why didn't he tell me?" The agonised question was for herself, not for Drew, but he answered, his voice dry,

"Only you know the answer to that."

She didn't want to answer that question, and there was another pressing for a reply. "Why are you doing this Drew? You don't even like Jon."

The tall dark figure lost a little of its assurance. "I like you Julia, I like you a lot. If things had been different," he shrugged his shoulders, "who knows?"

Julia jumped up, pulling his head down to kiss his cheek. "Drew, thank you." At least he understood: but would Jon?

She had to go to him, not to plead for his love but for his forgiveness. Drew smiled briefly. "I'll let myself out. Good luck."

★ ★ ★

The boat was in darkness. Julia let herself in, flicked the light on and looked into the empty galley. Jon wasn't in the bathroom either, although his shirt was soaking in the washbasin.

The bedroom was unoccupied too, his dinner-jacket lying in a crumpled heap on the bed. Julia picked it up, holding it to her cheek as an overpowering wave of love for Jon washed through her. Where was he? It had been a nasty cut, he shouldn't be wandering round in the dark after having it stitched.

She had to tell him what was behind Drew's toast in the restaurant. More important, she had to tell him she knew everything he'd done had been for her. She was prepared for the rejection which would follow, — there was no hope for them now — but realism didn't help the pain.

How long would he be? Julia made a cup of coffee, then left it untasted as she fidgeted about the saloon looking for something to read. She picked up the Omar Khayyam, then put it back, the memory was too painful.

She needed something light, frivolous, perhaps there was a magazine on the bureau.

There were some technical drawings, a three day old *Financial Times*, and on top of it a pile of letters in airmail envelopes. Julia picked them up to get at the newspaper then saw her name and address written in Jon's emphatic black handwriting. Puzzled, she shuffled through the pile. They were all addressed to her, unsealed, unstamped, unposted.

Breathlessly she began to read, sinking to the floor as the words and the intensity of their emotion hit her.

My dearest love, if only I could be sure you were happy, that I've done the right thing in keeping quiet, not telling you how much I love you. I'll never forget the look in your eyes as we made love. It scared me, terrified me. How could I ever live up to that trust, that openness? I'd always been a loner, never needed anyone,

*anything but my work. I was afraid
of the commitment, of letting you
down . . .*

Julia bit her knuckles hard, fighting
back the tears. She had to read on,
though it was breaking her heart to
see what she'd lost.

*. . . It's not easy being with Danny
all day, every day. I can't feel
ashamed of what we did, the way
I feel about you, even though you
are his wife now. Why couldn't I
accept responsibility for your love
when I had the chance, when you
were willing to give it to me? Will
you ever forgive me for running
like that? It was only afterwards I
realised how rejected you'd feel. But
it's too late now, you're in love with
Danny . . .*

How blind she'd been, but he'd
never given any sign of the depth of
his feelings. Why hadn't she trusted
her instincts, known it couldn't have

250

been like that for them without love?

Page after page rustled to the floor as she read, the tears running unheeded down her cheeks. Jon had poured out his heart in letters he could never post, laid himself open believing no one would ever see the words he'd needed so desperately to say.

Jon stood silent in the doorway watching Julia's burnished head bent over the last letter. The pale apricot skirt pooled round her, the letters like a drift of leaves on the faded carpet. He willed her to look up so he could read her face, know how she was reacting to his words.

Now the impossible had happened, she was reading, learning his true feelings for her, now when it was too late and he'd driven her into the arms of Drew Scott.

He must have made a sound. Julia's head came up and he saw the tears streaking her cheeks, the pain blurring her hazel eyes. In a moment he was on his knees beside her, gathering her into his arms, holding her close.

"I love you Julia," his voice was husky in her ear. "Don't turn to Scott, please forgive me . . . "

"Forgive you?" she asked incredulously, twisting to stare into his face. "How can I ever make up for what I've done to you?"

"By telling me the truth. Do you love Drew Scott?"

"No! I love you, I've always loved you Jon," her arms were fierce around his chest, as though she would never let him go. "I've been so stupid Jon, blind to what everyone else could see . . . "

Her lips sought his, grazing along his cheek until they fastened in blind supplication on his mouth, once hard and uncompromising, now pliant and responsive. "I love you, I love you," each whispered against the other's skin, drowning in the kiss, needing to submerge the betrayals of the past in an affirmation of love.

Jon deepened the kiss hungrily, as if he could never get enough of her and

252

all the time he was whispering words of love.

Her hands slipped under his loose sweatshirt, pressing him against her, desperate to be part of him for ever.

Jon's mouth left hers to imprint kisses along the pulse line of her throat, behind her ears, in her hair. There was all the time in the world for this moment of love and all the ones to come.

He scooped her up in his arms as effortlessly as if she'd been a child. "I've waited too long for you my darling, I want you in my bed, where you should have been a long time ago."

"Yes Jon."

"Tell me why," he teased, his voice smoky with desire.

"Because I love you, because I need you."

In the light from the bedside lamp he saw her dark pupils dilate with apprehension. "What is it, my love?" His eyes, black with intensity of his feeling searched her face with a tenderness that constricted her breath in her throat.

She shook her head, seeking the words. "It feels like the first time."

"It is the first time. The first time we've *made love*." And he began to show her.

★ ★ ★

Julia lay, her eyes closed, Jon's long body warm against hers. "No!" she protested as she moved to sit up.

Jon leaned on his elbow and laughed down into her face. "We can't stay like this all night my love."

"Why not? And call me that again.

"My love, my love," he repeated. "Now may I get up?"

"Why?"

"My hand hurts like hell and you're lying on it! Besides, we need to talk." Jon plumped up the pillows at the head of the bed, pulling her up to rest in the crook of his arm.

"I don't want to talk! I don't want to think about anything but here and now!"

"Julia darling, what's the matter? You know I love you, nothing in this world can change that."

All her insecurities came pouring out. "But the world hasn't changed! You're still going off to Brazil for months on end, and after that somewhere else. I can't live on letters Jon, not loving you the way I do."

He went very still. "And that's why you turned to Drew Scott."

"No! That was all part of Drew's scheme to make you jealous . . . "

"He succeeded in that."

"Good!" Julia retorted. "It hurt when you made a great show of not caring who I slept with. Drew was trying to bring us together."

Jon groaned. "I knew that man was too good to be true. Why on earth would he ruin his chances with you?"

"Because he recognised that all he'd ever be to me was a friend."

He ran his hands through his hair. "I couldn't be that self-sacrificing, not where you're concerned my darling. But forget Drew, I want to talk about us. Marry me Julia." The look on his face was so full of love she almost yielded. Then she thought of what it would be like, long months of loneliness, making a home he'd share only fleetingly, living their lives from leave to leave.

"I can't do it Jon. I want someone to wake up next to, someone to build a life with. I want a family . . . that's why I agreed to marry Danny. I wasn't in love with him, he knew that, but he thought it would be a good arrangement for both of us, and believing I could never have you . . ."

He pulled her tight against him, speaking into her hair, "It's all right, you don't have to tell me now. All that matters is that you're here and we love each other. You can have all the things you want my love — don't you think I want them too? I'll give up the foreign work . . ."

256

"No!" She twisted free to confront him, eyes sparking. "You can't do it, you'd hate it. And the first row we had, you'd throw it in my face — and I wouldn't blame you!"

"Let me finish! Max offered me the Brazilian project or a new post — as head of European Operations. I told him Brazil because I didn't think there was any hope for us, but the European offer's still open."

"But you'd hate being desk-bound!"

"I wouldn't be, there's some travelling involved, but for days not months. Don't you think I'm sick of impermanence, of crummy hotels, living out of suitcases or camping in the middle of nowhere? It was different fifteen years ago, I wanted the freedom. But," his voice was suddenly husky, "I don't want to be free any more, I want to be tied to you."

Julia couldn't stop the tears welling in her eyes.

"Have a hanky," he produced one from under the pillow. "See, I love you enough to marry you despite your funny red nose when you cry . . . "

"Jon!" she protested, crying and laughing at the same time. "Do you really mean it about the job?"

"Yes I mean it," he kissed her forehead. "Actually, it's all lies — I'm only marrying you because the European office will need a good personnel officer."

Julia looked up into the unmistakable love and laughter in his face. "Make love to me again Jon," she prompted softly, "then see if I believe you."

THE END

WITH SOMEBODY ELSE
Theresa Charles

Rosamond sets off for Cornwall with Hugo to meet his family, blissfully unaware of the shocks in store for her.

A SUMMER FOR STRANGERS
Claire Hamilton

Because she had lost her job, her flat and she had no money, Tabitha agreed to pose as Adam's future wife although she believed the scheme to be deceitful and cruel.

VILLA OF SINGING WATER
Angela Petron

The disquieting incidents that occurred at the Vatican and the Colosseum did not trouble Jan at first, but then they became increasingly unpleasant and alarming.

DOCTOR NAPIER'S NURSE
Pauline Ash

When cousins Midge and Derry are entered as probationer nurses on the same day but at different hospitals they agree to exchange identities.

A GIRL LIKE JULIE
Louise Ellis

Caroline absolutely adored Hugh Barrington, but then Julie Crane came into their lives. Julie was the kind of girl who attracts men without even trying.

COUNTRY DOCTOR
Paula Lindsay

When Evan Richmond bought a practice in a remote country village he did not realise that a casual encounter would lead to the loss of his heart.

ENCORE
Helga Moray

Craig and Janet realise that their true happiness lies with each other, but it is only under traumatic circumstances that they can be reunited.

NICOLETTE
Ivy Preston

When Grant Alston came back into her life, Nicolette was faced with a dilemma. Should she follow the path of duty or the path of love?

THE GOLDEN PUMA
Margaret Way

Catherine's time was spent looking after her father's Queensland farm. But what life was there without David, who wasn't interested in her?

HOSPITAL BY THE LAKE
Anne Durham

Nurse Marguerite Ingleby was always ready to become personally involved with her patients, to the despair of Brian Field, the Senior Surgical Registrar, who loved her.

VALLEY OF CONFLICT
David Farrell

Isolated in a hostel in the French Alps, Ann Russell sees her fiancé being seduced by a young girl. Then comes the avalanche that imperils their lives.

NURSE'S CHOICE
Peggy Gaddis

A proposal of marriage from the incredibly handsome and wealthy Reagan was enough to upset any girl — and Brooke Martin was no exception.

A DANGEROUS MAN
Anne Goring

Photographer Polly Burton was on safari in Mombasa when she met enigmatic Leon Hammond. But unpredictability was the name of the game where Leon was concerned.

PRECIOUS INHERITANCE
Joan Moules

Karen's new life working for an authoress took her from Sussex to a foreign airstrip and a kidnapping; to a real life adventure as gripping as any in the books she typed.

VISION OF LOVE
Grace Richmond

When Kathy takes over the rundown country kennels she finds Alec Stinton, a local vet, very helpful. But their friendship arouses bitter jealousy and a tragedy seems inevitable.

CRUSADING NURSE
Jane Converse

It was handsome Dr. Corbett who opened Nurse Susan Leighton's eyes and who set her off on a lonely crusade against some powerful enemies and a shattering struggle against the man she loved.

WILD ENCHANTMENT
Christina Green

Rowan's agreeable new boss had a dream of creating a famous perfume using her precious Silverstar, but Rowan's plans were very different.

DESERT ROMANCE
Irene Ord

Sally agrees to take her sister Pam's place as La Chartreuse the dancer, but she finds out there is more to it than dyeing her hair red and looking like her sister.

HEART OF ICE
Marie Sidney

How was January to know that not only would the warmth of the Swiss people thaw out her frozen heart, but that she too would play her part in helping someone to live again?

LUCKY IN LOVE
Margaret Wood

Companion-secretary to wealthy gambler Laura Duxford, who lived in Monaco, seemed to Melanie a fabulous job. Especially as Melanie had already lost her heart to Laura's son, Julian.

NURSE TO PRINCESS JASMINE
Lilian Woodward

Nick's surgeon brother, Tom, performs an operation on an Arabian princess, and she invites Tom, Nick and his fiancé to Omander, where a web of deceit and intrigue closes about them.